AN ORPHANAGE
OF DREAMS

Also by Sam Savage

AN ORPHANAGE
OF DREAMS

Sam Savage

COFFEE HOUSE PRESS
Minneapolis
2019

Coffee House Press books are available to the trade through our
primary distributor, Consortium Book Sales & Distribution, cbsd
.com or (800) 283-3572. For personal orders, catalogs, or other
information, write to info@coffeehousepress.org.

Coffee House Press is a nonprofit literary publishing house. Support
from private foundations, corporate giving programs, government
programs, and generous individuals helps make the publication of
our books possible. We gratefully acknowledge their support in detail
in the back of this book.

LIBRARY OF CONGRESS CATALOGING-IN-PUBLICATION DATA

Names: Savage, Sam, 1940– author.
Title: An orphanage of dreams / Sam Savage.
Description: Minneapolis : Coffee House Press, 2019.
Identifiers: LCCN 2018027628 (print) | LCCN 2018028475
    (ebook) | ISBN 9781566895392 | ISBN 9781566895309
    (trade pbk.)
Classification: LCC PS3619.A84 (ebook) | LCC PS3619.A84 A6
    2019 (print) | DDC 813/.6—dc23
LC record available at https://lccn.loc.gov/2018027628

PRINTED IN THE UNITED STATES OF AMERICA

25 24 23 22 21 20 19 18   1 2 3 4 5 6 7 8

Contents

AN ORPHANAGE
OF DREAMS

An Affair of the Heart

You never see Sue without Cleary. Even grocery shopping, which she does every Saturday, same as always, Cleary will be right beside her, pushing the cart. Sue is a deliberate shopper, she doesn't hurry, and she understands how to stretch a budget. She lingers over labels, compares prices, sorts coupons, feels fruit for soft spots, sniffs fish for freshness, thumps melons, and talks the whole time, an unbroken stream of bright prattle, descanting on the pros and cons of the various items, while Cleary, big hands gripping the handle of the cart, gazes blankly around the store. They don't exchange many words with each other anymore. It's hard to see why they are still together. You couldn't think of two people more different. Sue—small, animated, pointy-nosed, and birdlike—is chronically cheerful in a high-pitched way that strikes some people as overdone. She chirps, and her hands flutter like a pair of excited sparrows. Cleary, on the other hand, is tall and angular, with a thin face, a long nose, and a lower lip that protrudes in a constant pout that gives an incongruous childlike twist to the visage, softening the general dourness with a hint of melancholy. In conversation he tends to preface his meager portions of talk with a few seconds of weighted silence, as if pondering whether he oughtn't just end it right there. His hands are usually in his pockets or hanging at his sides.

Despite the flighty mannerisms, Sue has always been, except for that one time, a staunch, reliable, predictable woman. Elected secretary-treasurer of the Civic Club seven years running, she has yet to miss a Wednesday night meeting, while Cleary, as everybody knows, is the least civic-minded person around. He still complains bitterly about the fee for garbage pickup, refusing to acknowledge any advantage over the way they used to do it, when everybody drove his own trash out to the county dump. Even so, he has not let his low opinion of collective endeavor hinder him from chauffeuring Sue to the Wednesday night meetings at the town hall annex or from sitting in the car out front until the meeting is over, sitting there for over two hours listening to the radio and smoking and thinking God knows what. It's not as if Sue were incapable of driving herself. There was a time when she drove herself everywhere, you would see her all over town in the little red Toyota that just sits in the yard now, parked between the house trailer and a tumbledown shed where chickens used to live, tires pretty much rotted off it.

When they were first married and starting a family, Sue and Cleary wanted to do everything themselves, live the way people used to, keeping chickens and bees and a big garden, Sue pickling and canning what they couldn't eat at the time. Cleary built sheds and fences, sank a well, and erected a windmill of his own design to irrigate the garden. They even had goats for a time, when the children were small, because Sue thought goat's milk was better for them than cow's milk. But as the years went by they gave up farming, abandoned it bit by bit without any fuss or ever saying that this was what they were doing. First the chickens went and then the goats and bees. The windmill broke and Cleary never got around to fixing it. Row by row the garden dwindled, shrank to just a square patch of five or six tomato plants, until last year there was nothing.

The whole little farm is just one big lawn now. Driving past, you don't see them in the yard anymore, except sometimes Cleary out walking behind a power mower. The kids, a boy and a girl, are young teenagers now, well behaved and respectful, people say, but on their own most of the time. You don't see the parents at the Fourth of July picnic, or at football games either, though they still show up together for Sunday services at the United Methodist church in town. They get themselves there even in the worst weather, when the road down from their place is a toboggan run of slippery clay, though neither of them has any firm beliefs of a religious texture or strong urges in that direction. Sue goes because she feels better afterward. Listening to the sermon, reciting the Lord's Prayer in unison with others, and singing hymns in a small clear voice make her feel she is part of a larger, kinder world. Cleary goes because Ronny White is there.

Years ago, when the children were small, Sue and Ronny, who was also married with children, had a sudden brief and public love affair that tore Cleary up. One day, with nobody suspecting anything, they ran off together, just drove off one school-day morning, and the next thing any-body knew they were in Montana. When that happened Cleary's first impulse was to pack up and leave everything. He wanted to burn the house down, take the kids and dis-appear. But he couldn't, the shock and pain left him para-lyzed, he couldn't do anything but put one big foot in front of the other. He took the children to stay with his mother and went on as before, showed up every morning at the lumberyard, horsed around with the guys there same as before, and all the while he was burning with hurt and shame. One day Ronny's wife drove out to see him, because they were in it together she said, but he wouldn't talk to her, the pain was so great he couldn't look at it, if he had tried to talk the words would have choked him. Five months passed in that way and then one day Ronny was back, and eight days after that Sue came home too, riding the Greyhound all the way from Montana. She had tele-phoned Cleary from out there late one night, and he had told her she ought to come back.

That was more than nine years ago. They almost didn't survive. She had left him, left her two little kids. The kids are in high school now, and if they remember anything about that time they don't let on, and Sue and Cleary have never talked about it with them. They never talked about it with each other, they just picked up where they had left off, as if the five months that Sue was gone had never existed. What was there to say? The fact is she came back from Montana because Ronny had walked out on her there, came back with her tail between her legs, Cleary thought, though he never said that to her, not in those words.

On the outside Cleary was the same as before, but inside like a constant bright flame was the knowledge that she had never loved him in the way she loved Ronny. If she had already had kids by somebody else when she and Cleary had first met, she would never have left them for him, there was no way she would have left them. There were times, in the first years after she came back, when he wanted to grab her by the shoulders and shake her and shout, *Love me, you've got to love me.* But he knew it was no use, he couldn't reach inside her and get hold of whatever it was that constituted love and turn it back in his direction, and the impossibility of doing this drove him almost crazy, his own love was so strong, and yet it was not able to affect anything, couldn't make anything happen. Once when he was still a kid he had tried to move a chair with his thoughts. He had sat on the sofa in his parents' living room and looked at the chair, looked at it hard, and in his thoughts commanded it to move. He hadn't said any words out loud, but in his head he could hear his thoughts shouting, *Move, move.*

That Montana thing is an old story now. There ought by rights to be some days when he doesn't have to think about it, but there aren't any days like that. Sundays are the worst, he can't take his eyes off Ronny sitting there in a front pew next to his wife and kids as if nothing had ever happened. The rage still boils inside him, and seeing Ronny's blond head bowed in church he wants to crawl over the pews and pound him into the ground. If that ever actually happens, he knows he won't stop until he has pounded him under the earth.

It's all in the past now, he knows that, but the past is killing him. It's not the memory of the event itself, of the fact that Sue ran off to Montana, it's the memory of the pain it caused that is killing him. Nothing will ever be right unless he can go back in time and wipe the pain out, make it so it never happened, so he never felt it. But even God can't do that. God can't reshape the past any easier than Cleary can reshape Sue's love just by wanting. It's the impotence of desire that's killing him, sitting there like a fool, trying to make a chair move. He read in the paper a few years back about a man who was suffocated by a Volkswagen, and he never forgot the story. The man was under the car working on it when a jack gave way and the car came down on him. It didn't crush him, didn't break a single rib, but the weight of it settled on his chest and slowly suffocated him. Cleary thought about the man lying under the car, imagined him trying to push it off, pushing as hard as he could, harder than any man could normally be expected to push, and the car not moving.

Crocodiles and Parasols

1.

The scene: a wide river, sluggish, muddy, some kind of estuary. It is in Africa probably. On both sides of the river, or estuary, a sandy desert stretches away as far as the eye can see. No trees, not even palm trees, dot the landscape. In the beginning, a group of children, boys and girls, dressed in sailor suits and pinafores, are playing, or attempting to play, in the sand. But the sand is extremely fine and dry, almost a dry powder, and they are able to construct only formless piles like anthills. In the face of repeated failures, sweating in their city clothes, the children become quarrelsome and listless, some one and some the other, the quarrelsome ones striking the listless ones sharply in the face or dumping handfuls of hot sand down their shirts, the listless ones lying down in the sand, weeping softly. (They will remember this later.) The grown-ups, meanwhile, men and women whose children these presumably are, also dressed in dark city clothes, the men with top hats and canes, the women with parasols and bustles and exaggerated bosoms, stand in little clusters on the bank, cluster in little stands there, like trees in a landscape without any, and discuss whether the darkish things they see far out in the river are logs, almost submerged after months in the water, or crocodiles. The discussion is tedious, anfractuous, inconclusive. In their heart of hearts, they all, adults and children, would like just to dive in and get it over with.

2.

In the desert. A woman with two men. A man with two women. A boy, one of the crowd of children, is lying on his back in the hot sand, sweltering in his dark blue sailor suit. A man and a woman look down at him, eyes filled with pity, and then glance quickly at each other. The boy will remember this later. He will recall that glance as somehow "inestimably peculiar." The man is the man with two women. The woman is the woman with two men. A complex web is being woven. There is also a woman with a cat, and two women with one dog. They fight. The man and the woman who had been looking down at the boy, it could be a lifetime ago, draw apart from the others, to stand together, but not touching, on the sandy bank of the river. Behind them, sounds of continuous quarreling. Looking out at the water, speaking to the man, though not turning her head to face him, the woman says in a voice without inflection, and yet, for this very reason, charged with meaning, "Through the desert of tedium flows a river of dread." Horrified, the man realizes that this is true.

3.

The sand has become deeper. It is pulverous, like powdered talc. They sink ankle deep in it; it fills their shoes when they walk. The men and the boys have on socks of black silk, and the sand has infiltrated the cuffs. At first only a little sifted in, but gradually the opening at the top of the cuffs widened as the socks sagged, letting in more sand with each step they took. Now the socks hang in elephantine bulges around their ankles, and they walk with stumbling shuffles like men in shackles. Even the most optimistic among them knows that if the floating things in the river are crocodiles, they will not be able to escape. The women have taken off their shoes. Beneath the long dark dresses with bustles and jabot blouses, they wiggle their toes and remember walking barefoot in Deauville, and they remember how different the sand there was, how coarse and cool, though in the water there were sharks, concealed, swimming in patient circles beneath the waves. The people, the men and the women, even the most vociferous, are no longer talking. It is clear to everyone that argument is futile, and that the time for communion, if it ever existed, has now passed. The sun has reached the zenith, brilliant, blinding, unbearable. The men have removed their dark coats, dropping them in the sand at their feet. Now they take off their shirts and wrap them around their heads. The women have opened their blouses. They open and close the sides of their blouses, fanning their bare chests. The only shade is cast by the parasols, which the women hold just inches above their heads. The children, desperate, perhaps already dying, have crawled under the women's skirts. There in the mysterious dark, like the darkness in the churches at home, they kneel in the sand, and the bare legs of the women, rising up into the strange obscurity above, are like the columns of cathedrals. The men want to draw close to the women, to shrink into the shadows of their parasols, but they do not dare. Even now they do not dare. And when darkness finally comes, and all of consciousness is focused on a single sense, they become aware of the sound of the river behind them, the very faint liquid whispering of water against the bank. They turn, singly, and move toward the sound. The sand reaches above their knees. They struggle through it like travelers floundering in deep snow.

Balloons

By rights Amanda would have been the one in the balloon with Norman. Norman at the helm, if that is what it is
called, and Amanda leaning on the rail or rim or whatever
that is called, and waving to the crowd below. He would
have worn his captain's hat, and she would have had on
the gold-sequined gown she bought for the gala but never
got to wear, thanks to Genevieve. She was already in the
gown, was in front of the mirror adjusting the tiara, when
Genevieve burst in and said gleefully in front of everyone,
"Amanda will not be going to the ball."

Though she would not be going up in the balloon this time,
Amanda was comforted by the knowledge that neither
would Genevieve. And there would be other balloons for
Amanda, other days, perhaps even other Normans, while
Genevieve would not even see a balloon again unless she
had her eye at the air hole in the dungeon or oubliette, or
whatever it is called, when one went floating by.

Only boys were allowed in the balloon. When we peered
into the hangar and saw the sign "No Girls Aloft," we

adjourned to Millie's room and talked about getting even. Genevieve, who was still a member, gave a talk on sex as a weapon. Amanda showed off her new hat. Clara and Bibi got tangled in a lover's knot while everyone took pictures. Genevieve stormed out.

There was a great cry from outside. We clumped at the window. From below we looked like a bouquet of flowers, Norman said later. The boys had the balloon out on the lawn. Norman waved his captain's hat, and they loosed the anchor ropes. The balloon floated up, and there was Genevieve striding from the house. She stood on the lawn in a tangle of cast-off ropes and waved them up, and now they were waving down at her as she grew smaller and smaller. This was a picture none of them forgot: Genevieve in a white frock, on tiptoe, waving a small white handkerchief. Everyone's heart broke at once.

The age of flight had dawned. People lost interest in stuffed birds and waltzes. Amanda could not imagine anything more colorful than a balloon or anybody more colorful than Norman. The passion for the Montgolfier was greater than any passion before it. The orchestra played tangos, the balloons rose into the sky and disappeared behind the turrets, and at night they heard the guns.

Our generation was scarred by the balloons, by their ascent and their crashes, our hopes lifted and dashed. They crashed on their own or were made to crash by people shooting up at them. The broken balloons lay everywhere. They hung from trees and lay like wrinkled skins on the lawns. Peter took to drink, and Millie disappeared in a cloud of marijuana.

Norman came back. The bill of his captain's hat had been shot away. He had lost his color. Amanda led him, a small gray man, to fetch Genevieve from the dungeon. They showed her the presidential pardon, and she wept. Millie came out of her cloud and found them still there sitting on the old broken sofa. They thought they would move to one of the southwestern states. Norman flew over Arizona and reported back: the shadows there are like house cats, he said, and there is nowhere to hide.

The Awakening

I know why I came. I don't know why I stay.

I was on the point of departure when I began to stay. I made many attempts at leaving afterward, but I never again got so close that I could honestly say I was on the point of departure.

I sometimes blame the toaster oven. I really ought to have thrown it out at the very beginning, when I saw it would not turn off automatically and would have to be watched constantly, while there was still hope of getting a new one. I suppose I had scruples. It was not my job to throw out other people's small appliances. I went on using it instead, but was assiduous about pulling the plug afterward, sometimes returning to the kitchen to double or even triple check.

A bright side to my current situation is that I am now unlikely to leave the house with the toaster oven on, as I feared for a moment I was about to do.

I mean I am unlikely to leave the house.

I had already opened the front gate. Clutching a suitcase in each hand, I was about to step through to the street, when I remembered the toaster oven. I stood stock-still, while I tried to recall if I had unplugged it, a mental effort that is sometimes described as "ransacking the mind." From my experience of other people, including people in films, in similar situations, I assume that my expression at that moment was completely blank.

Imagine a man in his midforties, dark hair, of average good looks, though perhaps thinner than is considered healthy, standing in front of an open gate with a small pack on his back, a heavy suitcase in each hand, and a blank look on his face. He is wearing jeans, sandals, a Hawaiian shirt. The sun is shining. It is summer.

Standing there, ransacking, I was able to recall almost every instant of the morning—snapping shut the two suitcases I had packed the night before, checking the window locks, sweeping the crumbs of toast from the kitchen table, and after finishing my coffee, rinsing the cup and pouring the remainder of the milk down the drain. But when it came to the toaster oven, I drew a complete blank.

Picture a blackboard covered all over with writing except for a spot near the bottom where there's a broad whitish smudge made by an eraser.

There was nothing to do but check.

I realize now how absurd that was. Instead of checking I could have just left, stepped right through the gate into the street and on down the slope of departure. I could have caught an afternoon train to Marseille and from there taken a plane back to America. I could have rented a car in Nice, driven to Milan, and grabbed a flight to Tokyo. I could have worked my way down to San Rafael and Genoa, taken a room in the latter city, and begun research on a book about Columbus.

That's easy to see now.

I set down the bags and closed the gate. The latch, it seems to me now, fell with a dull thud. It fell with a small click.

I ran back up the stone stairway that climbed from the gate up through the terraced garden to the front door, pausing on the next-to-top step to bend and retrieve a key from a little crevice underneath, where I had placed it a minute before and where I had found it at the beginning of my visit.

I had expected, when I reached for the key at the start of my visit, a heavy old-fashioned key of a kind that I imagined was still common in France. But it was a Yale key of a type that is found everywhere.

I say *visit,* but of course as things have turned out it really cannot be considered a visit. A stay, I suppose, or a sojourn.

I bounded through the front room and the dining room and down the hall to the kitchen, which occupies a wing of its own at the rear of the house. The cord lay in neat coils on the counter next to the toaster oven. I no sooner saw it than I remembered coiling it in just that way.

I was turning back when I noticed a smudge on the little glass door of the appliance. I tried to take it off with my thumb, but that only made it worse. I remember thinking that I would just have to leave it like that, even as I went about dampening a sponge with detergent and scrubbing it clean. I don't understand why I did that.

I had been late for the bus already, and now instead of racing for the door, I stopped in the front room to gaze out a window. I moved a chair to one side in order to pull open the casements, push out one of the shutters, and look down. I saw the walk and the gate below me, and my suitcases standing side by side in front of the gate. There was something oddly moving, even mysterious, about the arrangement of things: the walkway paved with blue tile and bordered by gray-green dagger-leafed yuccas and yellow-flowering cacti, the white-painted wooden gate, and the two incongruous suitcases. I was reminded of a surrealist painting, by Magritte perhaps, or de Chirico, the way all the elements conspired to evoke the person who ought to be standing there between the suitcases but who was, mysteriously, missing. It was like seeing myself gone.

I heard the bus pulling away from the stop at the corner. I listened while it labored up the hill, the noise of its motor ascending from groan to whine and falling back to groan as it climbed a ladder of gears to vanish suddenly into silence. A silence that began, I suppose, with the driver lifting his foot from the accelerator at the moment the bus topped the ridge and started to coast down the far side, toward the Mediterranean and Nice in the distance. A foot in a regulation black shoe at the base of a blue-uniformed trouser leg, a shoe hinged on its heel, the toe slightly raised: and from there, from that minute motion, the lifting of the toe from the accelerator pedal, it—the silence—came rolling back in a vast cumulating wave over me and the house and the garden.

I recall feeling something very odd and intense. I was acutely aware of myself standing there at the window and looking down at my bags planted side by side on the sun-lit tiles, between the rows of desert vegetation, the spiked leaves and spines and the flowers that were too yellow, in front of the closed gate.

I stood there a long time. Dark clouds had begun to float in from the west. Fearing rain, I went down and brought the bags up.

Shortly afterward several drops fell, so few they made scarcely a sound, while dark splotches the size of nickels appeared on the walk. Then, a little later still, the sun came back out.

Wee People

They are extremely small. I hadn't thought people came that little. I can't help but think of them as "wee people," even though that conjures up images of leprechauns and such, which they don't at all resemble. If anything they resemble tiny bankers. That's because of the little pinstripes and the black umbrellas they all seem to carry with them even when there is no threat of rain. "Wee British bankers" I think pretty well sums them up. Sums up their appearance, I mean, because they certainly don't *act* like bankers. Several months ago, for example, I came into the kitchen and found one of them standing on the counter next to the blender. The instant it caught sight of me it jumped to the floor, using its umbrella as a parachute. It shot right past me and a moment later I heard the front door slam. That was the first time I had found one in the house.

Silvia says they breed in the compost. I don't think so. She says that because she is angry about the second composter. "You and your rotting vegetables," she says, standing on the deck and pointing at my composters lined up next to the garage. "Is this a trailer park?" Of course she knows it's not a trailer park. An overreliance on the counterfactual interrogative—"Are you an idiot?" "Is that your underwear in the bathroom?"—is one of Silvia's tics. *Composting,* of course, has nothing to do with *rotting,* it is the work of thoroughly benign microorganisms, but when I try to explain that to her she just walks off or, if we are sitting, sticks her fingers in her ears. I don't think Silvia is aware of how annoying that is.

In addition to bacteria, I try to tell her, you need nitrogen, oxygen, water, and the right mix of protozoa, rotifers, molds, and of course earthworms; you have to have earthworms. You don't add them. They come on their own. Aristotle thought that all animals were born of other similar animals, except for flies, which he thought hatched spontaneously from dirt. Aristotle was not a composter or he would have believed the same of earthworms. The most rudimentary compost pile, left to itself for a few summer days, will slither with them. They just pop up. It's like a miracle, I tell Silvia. Now that I think about it, that must be what gave her the idea that little people can arrive in that way.

Silvia is not a gardener, to say the least. She won't even eat most of the things I grow. Of course eating them is not the point. I like being outside. Even when there's nothing to do in the garden, I prefer being there to sitting in the house listening to Silvia's friends. Sometimes I sit in the garage. I was in the garage when I heard the little people for the first time, heard their vocalizations, I mean; I can't say they were actually *talking.* I peeked out the window. A pair of little ones—small even by their standards—were standing beneath a tomato plant in the garden. They seemed to be bickering. There was a rapid exchange of high-pitched squeals accompanied by threatening gestures with the umbrellas. Though I can't say for certain that they were talking, the shrill vibrato chittering was exactly the way one would expect a very tiny language to sound—not just small in volume but composed of very tiny words. Sometimes when Silvia has her friends over and they are in the dining room all talking at once, I find myself listening away, so to speak, hearing the sounds but blocking out their meaning, and it was exactly like that—a shrill feminine chatter that, when listened to in that way, sounds exactly like squealing.

Silvia enjoys making heavy-handed sarcastic remarks about me and my "little friends," as she calls them. I usually manage to shrug those off, as I did just the other night. We had been watching the news on TV, when she abruptly leaned over and said in my ear, "Another politician in a sex scandal. What do your little friends think of *that*?" As if they could be bothered! I told her I doubted they would even know about it. I don't think they have newspapers.

There seem to be more and more of them. I know it sounds odd to speak of things that small as *massing*, but that is just what they appear to be doing. I saw them in ones and twos at first, usually in the garden, but lately I've noticed them in larger groups in the street out front. They seem to be talking about us, pointing the wickedly sharp tips of their little umbrellas at our house. I tried discussing this with Silvia, but she just walked off.

She is upset over the missing money, even storming outside to shout at me, leaning over the deck rail and yelling down at me while I am bent over in the garden weeding. I don't even look up when she does that. She is always losing money and then blaming other people. When I suggested that maybe the little people took it, she flew into a rage, screaming, "There *are* no little people." Which was a stupid thing to say.

Silvia has always earned more than me. Furthermore, she likes her job. I hated my job, could scarcely drag myself to work in the morning, and when the headaches started I would either have to go home or lock the door to my office and lie down on the floor. I liked getting home early and having the house to myself. So when I lost my position, I thought, why bother. Silvia was earning plenty for both of us. I thought I would do something creative, though I haven't settled on anything yet, except gardening. Silvia says she doesn't understand how I can sit around doing nothing. A remark like that tells you a lot about Silvia.

I don't know where they would keep the money if they took it. The pockets in their little suits would hold a few postage stamps at best, or a couple of dimes. But still they do *have* pockets and must use them for something. I wouldn't be at all surprised if they had their own tiny currency.

Silvia won't let it go, complaining, squealing, and now threatening to take steps. Bluster, probably, but I've begun taking photos of them, just in case. And they seem to enjoy that, putting on poses and doing tricks with the umbrellas, as if they want to appear in the very best light, as well they should.

Last week I found out that she had been putting down rat poison. I said to her, "Do you realize what you've done? They're not *mice*! They don't even *look* like mice." The minute she left for work, I went around the house and gathered up all the pellets I could find. I did the best I could, but I fear I was too late. I think they know.

Four nights ago we found a length of heavy twine stretched across the stairs, obviously calculated to send Silvia plunging down. She saw it just in time. Of course she was thoroughly shaken. She went into the bathroom and locked the door. I think I heard a sob.

I am worried about the bankers. Yesterday I saw several of them at the kitchen window looking out at me while I was weeding. Since I began sleeping in the tent, I've seen nothing of Silvia. I've heard the phone ringing. It rings a long time, stops, and then begins to ring again. There are no lights on in the house. It's possible that she has gone off somewhere, some place where she can rest, but I don't think so. When the police come, I'll show them the photographs.

Walter

"Walter is not well today," Marie-Claire told the assembled crowd, and she paused a moment before adding, "I'm sorry," as if *she* were responsible for whether Walter was well today, with the implication that she was somehow *in charge* of Walter. She had taken him on in a difficult period, that much was true, and of course we were all grateful to her for that, but answering correspondence and keeping an eye out for people coming in across the lawn were hardly tasks that gave her authority over his *person,* and one of us ought to have had the courage to stand up and say that to her face.

Of course Richard, for one, had said those things to her face countless times in the most abusive ways imaginable, accusing poor Marie-Claire of being a martinet and a shrew, among other things, but no one ever paid attention to Richard, Marie-Claire least of all. And I *would* have said them to her if she had not been so prickly about criticism from other women, holding us at arm's length, emotionally speaking, and acting as if we were all out to sink our hooks into Walter, as if in my case that would even be *possible.*

We had been waiting over an hour already, uncomfortable and shivering in the hard little folding chairs that Walter had brought in ages ago, after he had noticed that people were nodding off during the talks. In fact only a handful of people had been nodding off, chins on chests, one young man snoring a little, and that was not the fault of the cushy armchairs we had back then—they nodded off because they were on drugs, as was obvious to everyone but Walter, who was absorbed in his work and so isolated and spiritual he practically lived in another *universe*. In the old days, we used to drag and shove those heavy armchairs into a cozy circle around Walter, who would perch on a high wooden stool and just *talk* to us. By making us sit in folding metal chairs so hard and uncomfortable that after fifteen minutes you wanted to scream, Walter was in fact, without even *knowing* it, punishing everyone for the sins of a few, though of course no one pointed this out or even complained slightly, because everyone was afraid of Walter, except Marie-Claire, of course, and me, and Richard.

They had, as usual, turned the air-conditioning so low we must have looked like rows of *lumps* or *bundles* in our colorful hoods and parkas. It was kept that way for Walter's sake, so naturally we didn't complain; we just dressed appropriately. And of course the commotion from the people milling around outside was putting everyone on edge. The crowd had been out there in the sweltering heat for hours, and now some of them were shouting and banging at the doors, as if it were *our* fault they didn't have tickets. And meanwhile the people inside were fidgeting and squirming about on the metal chairs, trying to get comfortable, and some had stood up and were stamping and flexing their legs, fearing blood clots, none of us being really young anymore, and everybody just waiting for Marie-Claire to wheel Walter out. I had dropped by the lodge that very morning, thinking I might just as well bring Walter over, and Marie-Claire had told me he wasn't well. "Walter's in bad shape," was how she put it. A masseuse from the New Life Foundation was in with him, trying to work him into shape for the talk, and I was not to go in there, she said flatly. She used her foot to block the door from inside when I pushed, so I came on over alone, determined to raise the incident with Walter when he arrived.

I was wondering whose decision it had been to leave him behind the curtain all this time—and whether this was not just one more example of Marie-Claire's deciding things on her own despite having agreed years ago that important decisions would be made as a group—when Richard jumped to his feet and began shouting, "*Show* him to us, we want to *see* him." Everybody was thoroughly tired of Richard's outbursts, so most of us just studied our feet and pretended we didn't hear him, which was always a gamble with Richard—it would sometimes just enrage him. I am convinced he would have grabbed his chair and actually thrown it at Marie-Claire if Bill Ekman, sitting directly behind, had not planted both his big wingtips on the back rung. Richard was tugging at the chair and shouting, "We *want* to see him," over and over, when it dawned on him that something was fastening the chair to the floor. He looked down and saw Bill's big feet, and then he looked at Bill, who was staring straight ahead as if he didn't know anything about the feet. Richard gave the chair a final half-hearted tug and sat down. His face was bright red. Richard didn't belong there.

Meanwhile the chanting outside was growing louder. There were several tremendous thuds at the door, followed by cheers, as if they had found some sort of *ram* and intended to *batter* their way in. It was thoroughly wrong of Marie-Claire to post the conference online. At the last planning session, when it was already obvious there was going to be trouble, I asked her why in the world she had posted a private meeting online for all the world to see instead of just *mailing* the tickets the way we used to. I also pointed out once again how *useless* it was to put a keycode at the main gate if people could just come in across the lawn. "Well, that's how *Walter* wants it," she said, as usual.

Some in the crowd outside had climbed up the trellises and were now slapping the upper windows with the flats of their hands, a regular *tam tam tam*. There was a tremendous thud against the door and more cheers. In the face of this, Marie-Claire did the only thing she could do and pretended not to notice. She raised her voice and began reading what she claimed was a message from Walter, but of course I knew it was not an authentic message from Walter. Richard was grousing again, wagging his big head and mumbling to himself. I turned around and positively *hissed* at him. "I am trying to *concentrate*," I hissed, and he shut up.

Marie-Claire was talking about self-reliance. This was not on the program. I was thinking that here was just another example of Marie-Claire's high-handedness, when Denise interrupted. "Excuse me, Marie-Claire," she said, "self-reliance is not on the program," and she held the program up, turning it this way and that for everyone to see. Marie-Claire said, "Thank you, Denise, for pointing that out. I'll be sure to mention it to *Walter*," which was a *crushing* thing to say to Denise of all people, who never got to mention *anything* to Walter. Denise just smiled meekly, though I'm sure she wanted to scratch Marie-Claire's eyes out.

I wondered if Walter had overheard their exchange, and I reflected on how peevish we had all become lately. There was a time when no one ever said anything that did not make someone else feel *better*. Before coming here we had all been living in *holes,* as Walter called them, and we were always terrified he would catch us in some catty remark and make us stand up in front of everyone and take it back and go through the exercise he called *climbing out of the hole,* which was a terrible experience, even though one always felt better afterward.

The commotion outside and the pounding and banging at the windows and door were so loud I was convinced the back rows were not catching a word of what Marie-Claire was saying, and Richard had started up again, carrying on in an angry voice about her hiding Walter, and everyone was getting very nervous. If Marie-Claire had had an ounce of brain, we would have had extra security. There we were, under fire practically, with people pouring in across the lawn nearly every day, with Walter forced to rely on Marie-Claire for the smallest thing, and we had to make do with Belton, who was only marginally adequate when the worst we had to deal with was shoplifting from the gift shop. That very morning I had watched him lumbering across the grass in pursuit of two women half his age. I said to myself then that all we needed was for Belton to have a heart attack, and now I could just picture him outside in that crowd trying to pry people away from the door and being completely ineffectual, just one more item to bring ridicule on us.

I turned around and saw that Eileen had buried her face in her mittens, and I was sure it was because of the ridicule. Her husband was staring up at Marie-Claire. He seemed to be chewing on something thick; he looked stunned. No one had ever liked Marie-Claire, but we put up with her for Walter's sake. We had talked it over together when she first came, and we had made each other understand that Marie-Claire possessed a lot of sex appeal even for someone as advanced as Walter. Even so, it was hurtful to visit the lodge for our appointment and to sit there earnestly reporting on our progress and being chastised or encouraged, depending, and to realize that someone was in the shower, and then have her appear at lunch, sitting at his table with me and Richard and a few others who were allowed to sit there, damp hair and all, while Walter fawned over her, feeding her bits of food, and she with her chair pushed right up against his and her mouth open like a horrid little baby bird.

Of course we had all deteriorated since then, gone terribly downhill physically speaking; we were crumbling actually, though Walter, I was sure, had only increased in *wisdom,* and Marie-Claire had really *broadened,* was now as squat and round as a pickle jar; "like a penguin carrying two bags of silicone," was how Richard put it. Naturally we all *forgave* Walter, and we tried to like Marie-Claire, but we never could. That was especially true for those of us who had been there longest, Richard and myself and a few others. When she started recruiting all those new people for whom Walterism was just slogans, who thought a retreat was all about balloon rides and trips to Disneyland, we tried to put a stop to it, but it was no use if Walter would not get behind us.

Now Marie-Claire was asking everyone to *please* apply the skills we had learned from Walter, and some did try, closing their eyes and humming, but it was difficult with everyone else fidgeting and whispering, and Richard shouting again. I thought, "For God's sake, Marie-Claire, *bring him out.*" But at least the people outside had finally stopped banging. And then Bill Ekman stood up and pointed at the windows. "It's one hundred and fifteen degrees Fahrenheit outside," he said. "Those people are going to *die* out there." I looked up and saw the people at the windows were pressing their bare chests against the cool glass, and some of them were *licking* it. There was no sign of Belton. Everyone began to argue about the people outside, some wanting to let them in and others fearing that this would cause a stampede and urging us to think of *Walter,* but at least Richard, who had stood up also and was staring bug-eyed at the naked people plastered against the glass, had finally shut up.

Richard had a lot on his conscience. It had been his idea to bring the New Life Foundation in to work on Walter—a total waste of money, in my view. The lumps were still there, all over his body, and there were new ones on his neck. We were all so desperate and hopeful and really counting on Walter when we came here, each of us so *alone* then, on the verge of *suicide* most of us, and over the years we had become completely dependent on him. We found it impossible to even *think* about losing Walter. Without him there would be no hope for any of us—just solitude and longing and disappointment and hating ourselves. Sometimes, thinking about a future without Walter, I wanted to just get down on my knees and bang my head on the floor.

I was already up on the stage and had reached the curtain when I heard the glass shatter. I glanced back and saw them pouring in through the smashed door. The people inside were trying to hold them back, linking arms to form a barricade between them and Walter. Richard was shouting, "Save *Walter.*" People in down jackets and mittens were wrestling with people who were practically naked, and Marie-Claire was shrieking for everyone to *please* sit down.

I slipped behind the curtain. I looked down at Walter, who was slumped over, leaning heavily against an arm of the wheelchair, his poor head twisted at an awful angle, and my heart just froze. I knelt, took his head in my hands, lifted it gently. The eyes stared straight ahead; they were not even the right color, and I could tell they didn't see me. Bits of straw clung to his sweater. His right leg was just a mass of lumps. "Walter," I murmured, "what have they done to you?" And that was when I saw the opening at the base of his neck, a mouth-like gape. A tongue of white stuffing oozed from it. It must have happened when his head fell to the side. I thought, "*Damn* Marie-Claire."

I thought, "*Damn* her, *damn* her, *damn* her." I took Walter in my arms—he was no heavier than a large pillow—and carried him over to the little daybed. I laid him down gently. The shouting and banging beyond the curtain grew louder; they must have been throwing chairs; and I heard sirens in the distance. "This will be the end of us," I thought, and I lay down on the bed next to Walter. I put my arm under his head, cradling it, and tried to push the stuffing back in with my fingers. Marie-Claire came in behind the curtain and stopped dead in her tracks. She looked at me lying there in bed with my arms around Walter, and I could feel her just *withering*.

Animal Crackers

Muskrat

The muskrat is an important animal. It lives in holes. It seldom experiences any of the extreme forms of anxiety. It is not in holes because of that. It does not fear nuclear attack. It smells bad, hence the name. It smells good to other muskrats. We have no idea how it smells to other muskrats. At what point will we cease being fond of it? It used to be valued in coats. They were not called muskrat coats because that was too much like rat coats. It doesn't like being made into coats. It makes little stick houses on the ice. It is not a miniature beaver. It does not do well in college. Male muskrats engage in bloody combat over female muskrats. It does not mature easily. It must not be confused with the European water rat. It does not like moles.

Pangolin

It eats ants. It is not an anteater. Nobody seems to know what it is exactly. It is a scaly mammal. It prefers the simple life. When frightened it curls up into an impregnable ball. A frightened pangolin is the size of a basketball. If you puncture a pangolin, air does not come out. It is capable of making a hissing sound but that is not the reason. It possesses a thin, very sticky tongue that it uses to capture ants and termites. The tongue is so extremely long it is kept in a sheath that reaches to the pangolin's abdomen. When people have epileptic seizures it is important not to let them swallow their tongues. There are no epileptic pangolins. There are no photographs of Dostoyevsky with a pangolin. When Dostoyevsky was twenty-eight he was sentenced to be shot for sedition. He stood in the prison yard. He was in his underwear and it was very cold. They were to be shot three by three. He was in the second group of three. He was not allowed to curl up into a ball.

Porcupine

It hates its name. It is not a pig. It has piglike eyes. It can't jump. It is nearsighted, has a large brain and an excellent memory. Resentment builds up. It is lonely. It goes to the park by itself. It is always alone on its bench. It is prickly and no one wants to sit with it. It feels like a pig. It dreams of an address in Hollywood. Sometimes on dark nights it roosts in trees. It has a tiny apartment in a suburb of Cleveland, the most distant place it had money to get to. What a life. In the winter it eats conifer needles and bark. It is deeply pessimistic. It is more pessimistic than any animal before it. In the spring it eats flowers.

Wolverine

It is always angry. It takes medicine for this. It has tried meditation, long-distance running, yoga, nothing helps. It tried golf, but that made it angrier. It looks like a portly and well-fed bear though it is constantly afraid of starving. It is fond of moose. It is a noisy eater. It sits at the counter in the diner and people stare. It wears a brown soup-stained cardigan that it never washes. It complains to anyone who will listen. When it was still young it went off to London, because it wanted to improve itself. It found a room in Ealing. That was in 1963. It bought a trench coat. It tightened the belt across its belly and turned the collar up. It bought a hat. It made sandwiches and ate them in Hyde Park. It did not want to be recognized. One night it went to Covent Garden to see Margot Fonteyn dance with Rudolf Nureyev, who had just defected from the Soviet Union. It kept its hat on. People were looking at it. They were wondering what a wolverine was doing at Covent Garden. Nureyev danced. It was the most beautiful thing the wolverine had ever seen. It was so beautiful the wolverine began to cry, and the block of anger inside it melted and flowed away with the tears.

That was a long time ago. The Soviet Union is gone. Nureyev is gone. The wolverine is old, it has forgotten the forest, it has forgotten London, it sits at the counter, tears at its food, and complains.

Weasel

After work the weasel gets together with other weasels that hang out on the corner across from Eddie's Meat Market.

That's their corner, everybody knows it's their corner, polecats and stoats are not welcome. The weasels don't have a lot to say to each other, they just bitch and complain and leer at people walking past. Eddie at the market hates having them there, they scare customers off, he says, nobody wants to walk past a bunch of leering chicken killers. They hang out there anyway, out of spite, just to show him they are somebodies. The weasel doesn't give a damn about the other weasels' problems, he barely listens to their whining. It feels good to complain aloud after bottling it up all day at work, just saying the words feels good to him even if none of the others listen or would care if he dropped dead tomorrow. Afterward, at home in his burrow, he wonders if the others are as lonely as he is. It would be funny if they all really just wanted friendship and love and couldn't get any closer to it than standing around bitching on a street corner.

Klatsch

Their number fluctuated from week to week, but they were almost never fewer than three, three was the bottom limit. He could remember only a couple of times with just two. It was awkward when they were just two, hard to get a conversation going, and, once going, steer it in the right direction, keep it from collapsing into long awkward silences that only got worse with every second, until the awkwardness started to feel more like panic, until finally one of them, nearly desperate, would toss something out, any odd thing, it didn't matter. And it didn't matter which two it was, none of them had the sort of personality that held up well under those conditions, facing each other across a little table in a coffee shop, the usual topics didn't work under conditions like that. The conversation, the repartee, the jokes felt contrived, rehearsed, his own voice, he could hear, sounded stilted and insincere. When he saw it would be just two of them, his impulse was to call the klatsch off. But he couldn't actually do that. To even suggest such a thing, and explain why he thought it was a good idea, presupposed an intimacy that was not in the ethos of the klatsch, even though he was sure the other person felt the same way, was thinking the same thing. So they had to go through with it, had to sit there and chat in that painful stilted way for an hour or more, even though they were not enjoying it, when enjoying the company of others was the whole point of the klatsch. After the last time that had happened, when only Harv of all people had showed up, he had come up with the idea of a quorum rule. The next time they all got together he would ask them to make it a rule that, when only two people came, it was not to be considered a proper klatsch, in which case they could just go back home, turn on their heels and leave without any fuss or discussion, because that was the rule. But he didn't know how to tell the group that he wanted this, it was not the sort of thing they talked about in the klatsch, they were not close in that way, so he never brought it up. They kept it light, a lot of joking, sometimes a bit of good-natured teasing. There were no formal rules, but they all understood that nobody wanted heavy trips. Occasionally, it is true, they would turn on an absent member and gossip about him in a way that was sometimes vicious, but face-to-face they kept things amiable. He was never absent, the one person who had never missed a klatsch, because living alone, having no family nearby, he had nothing better to do on a Sunday morning. They met in either of a pair of coffee shops, in Jack's Java Joint two blocks east of his place or the Lighthouse three blocks west, so it was nothing for him to just walk over. The group was maybe ten people, counting the ones who came only now and then, with just five regulars, or six if you included Lena, who was semi-regular. It took a lot to keep the regulars away. On the day

38   Sam Savage

of the giant blizzard, four-foot drifts on the sidewalks and the city practically shut down, they were all five at Jack's, the only customers in there. Jack had opened the shop just for them, he was that sure they would show up. He made them coffee and pancakes with bacon or sausage, and when they had all been served he fixed a cup for himself and sat with them. They were men and women, they were of different ages, from different walks of life, a lineman for the electric company, a dog trainer, a middle-school music teacher, it was hard to say what they had in common. Maybe they didn't have anything in common and that was the point, was the thing that made the klatsch interesting, hearing the various perspectives people had. They never saw each other outside of the klatsch. He was the intellectual of the group, the news junkie, the one with the statistics. Being on disability he didn't have anything to do all day but read the papers and watch CNN. He liked knowing what happened the moment it happened. During big unfolding events like a hurricane or a hostage situation, he would get up in the night and turn on the computer to find out the latest. It always seemed to him that the others, who showed less interest in such things, were cutting themselves off from the world. He was often angered by things he read and saw, the lies of politicians, the cupidity and fraud of Wall Street, the ignorance and folly of people generally. He knew more than the others, had more facts ready at hand, and sometimes he worried that he might be going on for too long. Sometimes, reflecting on it afterward, he felt he had been too insistent or too forceful with his opinions. He sometimes lost control of his voice and could sound irritated and peevish without meaning to. No one became blatantly angry with him when he held forth for a long time or lost control of his voice, but he was aware of a kind of tension in the air, and thinking it over later he would wonder if they wouldn't be happier if he weren't part of the group, or maybe not part of it every Sunday. When he walked into Jack's a little after ten this morning he was surprised that none of the others were there yet. He got coffee, took his usual seat at the head of the long table by the window, and waited. He read the front page of the paper that he had already read at home. He guessed they were at the Lighthouse, he must have been distracted when they were deciding where to meet next, and so he walked over there, but they weren't at the Lighthouse either, and he came back to Jack's. He couldn't figure it out, it was eleven o'clock already. He decided to call. He never called, he didn't even have numbers for most of them, but he called the ones he had. Nobody answered. That wasn't surprising. A crisp, clear autumn morning, people had better things to do than sit in a stuffy coffee shop. That was normal, they weren't married to each other. Nobody came every Sunday. It was just a coincidence that they had all stayed away today, it was bound to happen eventually. He could have been one of them, he might well have found something else to do on a day like today, he might have gone for a long walk, he really ought to walk more, or for a drive in the country. He might have stopped for lunch in some little country town. That would really have been strange, if he had actually done that, the hour of the klatsch arriving and nobody there at all. He ordered an egg sandwich. He ordered the same thing every Sunday. They teased him about that, about being a stick-in-the-mud, he never ate an egg sandwich otherwise. The waiter set it down in front of him, a rye bread sandwich topped with a sliced pickle in a nest of potato chips, and he just looked at it. He didn't feel like an egg sandwich. He wished he hadn't come, he wished he had done like the others and just not showed up, it was stupid, he was always the odd man out. He studied his face in the window glass. He looked terribly tired, even depressed, he wasn't getting enough sleep. He didn't know how much longer he could go on like this. He was forty-eight years old, he had already had most of the life he was ever going to have. Seated at the head of the long empty table, he was conscious of looking ridiculous. If the others had showed up, if even one of them had thought to show up, the morning might have been different. *Fuck them,* he thought. *Fuck every goddamn one of them.* He got up to leave. He told Jack he wasn't hungry. Outside on the sidewalk, in the Sunday morning quiet, a cardinal balancing on a wire directly above him whistled clear and clean, the chill sunlight of early autumn flooded the street and ricocheted from the windshields of cars, the sky was blue and cloudless.

1. Wolves

It is not true that there are wolves in the city now. People hear the dogs howling and think they are hearing wolves. That's because the bigger dogs—the shepherds, the malamutes—sound like wolves, or the way they imagine wolves sounding. Most people have never heard actual wolves. It doesn't make a whole lot of difference, probably, whether they are actual wolves or not, as there are now reliable reports of people being eaten by dogs. Wilson stands in the doorway and stares out at the jungle. He wants us to stop calling it "the park." "There is nothing parklike about it," he grumbles loudly. Celia has not abandoned the search for more bullets. It won't be possible to kill them all with the bullets we have. We don't have even a hundred bullets.

2. Stanley

It had been a week since Sheila had heard from Stanley, so she decided to open the door and look. She could tell right away that he was dead. She went up and called the police.

They wanted to know if he had gotten into the dryer by himself. Sheila said, "How could he get in by himself?" Stanley had always hoped for a poem, and now he was dead.

Everything about Stanley was odd.

3. Buddies

They were walking single file, ten feet apart as they had been trained, to limit casualties, when Private Nolan stepped on an explosive device. Nolan lost both legs and died in the helicopter. Private Callaway, who was behind him, took shrapnel in the face. Everyone felt bad about Nolan. A year later, on the flight back to the States, they were still talking about him. Callaway was not well liked. He was generally regarded as a prick, and after he was evacuated to Landstuhl no one in the unit thought to mention him again. They never found out what happened to him later.

4. Dad

Whenever Dad came to visit, he ran the Cadillac up on the lawn, fitting it between the kids' swing set and the shack. He would open the car door and practically tumble out on the porch. He was not Rebecca's dad and she didn't like him driving on her grass. Jack was too busy painting to care. Dad stood next to Jack at the easel and criticized. Rebecca took Dad to look for swans by the lake so he wouldn't disturb Jack while he was painting. The kids came back from school and Dad gave them each a dollar. Then Rebecca and

Dad took them for ice cream so Jack could paint. When the kids grew up, all they could remember about Dad was that he had given them money and had run over their swing set. After Dad died, Jack gave up painting and moved back to the city. Rebecca spoke fondly of Dad, though the whole painting thing had been a nightmare.

5. Diebecker

They had packed up and were ready to move out when the courier arrived with the colonel's orders: they were to hold the sector at all costs. They all knew that this was a delaying tactic at best, meant to give the colonel time to catch a boat to America. They were in sad shape, with fewer than a hundred bullets. After ordering his men back to their posts, Lieutenant Diebecker sat beneath a tree and composed the poem we all know today. Private Schulz climbed on a chair and read it to the troops. It turned out not to be the moment. The sullen silence that followed the recitation prompted Diebecker to release the safety on his pistol. Later, as senator, he championed the idea of the well-read soldier.

6. The Funeral

The funeral was a great success. Calvin flew over in an airplane trailing one of Stanley's string poems. Everyone said it was hopeless. A woman in a fur coat brought a small dog. She sang a song she had written herself, which everyone thought was awful. Jared said Stanley was a light in a dark world, which everyone considered stupid. Peter came in his fire engine. He said that if Stanley had become a fireman, he would still be with us—he was always seeking new experiences, and now that had cost him his life. We did not have a minister and so were not sure when it was over. Peter had to get to the parade, so in the end we all climbed on the fire engine and rode at the front of the procession. Everyone thought of Stanley.

7. Max

One day, crazy with loneliness, Max got on a plane and flew to the Canary Islands. On his first day there he sat in a cafe with a view of the port. In the port were fishing vessels and cargo ships from all over the world. On the second day he rode on a tour bus around the island. The bus stopped at an overlook, and the passengers got down and stood at the railing. The guide told them that from here one could sometimes glimpse the Tenerife volcano appearing to float in the air above the horizon, though today it was obscured by haze. Some of the passengers on the tour complained about the haze, but not Max. On the third day he wrote a postcard to his landlady, who was the only person whose address he could remember. He told her the food for the cat would not last forever. On the fourth day he did nothing. On the fifth day he went to a bar crowded with tourists and made the acquaintance of an attractive woman from Italy. He made up several stories about his life in America. They drank till closing time and parted without exchanging addresses. "Ciao," she said, as her taxi pulled away. "Ciao," Max said. The next day he flew home. On the plane he fell into conversation with a Canadian man seated next to him. The Canadian told Max about the death of his Yorkshire terrier. His eyes welled with tears and he choked back a sob when he talked of the dog's suffering. Max felt embarrassed for him. He didn't like dogs, or animals in general other than cats, and he couldn't recall what a Yorkshire terrier looked like.

8. Old Pals

If we lived in villages we could go into the mountains to pray. We can't pray parked in a car like this. Somebody should help us. The police are not our friends. If we hadn't talked so much about revolution we wouldn't feel so bad now. Existentialism was an exciting philosophy then, but nobody reads those people anymore. We never thought, after all the anguish and all the struggles, that we would end up sitting in a car, all of us together, the two in front and the three in back, sometimes all five of us smoking at once. We keep the windows cracked. We are kidding ourselves. We were always kidding ourselves, kidding each other. We talked big but we weren't serious. At bottom we were not serious people. Big talkers, loudmouths. Or maybe just dreamers. I'd like to think we were just dreamers. "A lot of water over the dam," somebody says, and we all agree. A lot of goddamn water. All we have is each other. Sometimes we drive around for hours, smoking and talking. Nobody wants to go home.

9. Tools

He didn't have tools. There was no way he could fix the car without tools. Meanwhile the snow was getting deeper. If he took the engine apart he would have to be careful not to let any of the small pieces fall into the snow. If they fell into the snow he wouldn't see them again till spring. If he lost them in the snow, there was not going to be any spring for him. He could ask Wyman for tools. Wyman had a tool for everything. That would mean walking to Wyman's hut in the snow. He knew Wyman wasn't going to give him the tools. He never let anybody use his tools. He was worried they would get lost in the snow. If Max got to Wyman's hut he could stay there till spring. Wyman might lend him the tools then and he could fix the car and get out of here. Janet would be in Mexico by then. He would never find her there.

10. Doris and Harry

There are too many holes. It is mostly holes. We can't cross because of the holes. Imagine falling into one of the holes. What is at the bottom? Is there a bottom? Or do you go on falling forever? Doris stands with Harry at the railing. Harry is in a diving suit. They wonder if they will see each other again. It won't make a difference one way or the other. Harry will not be the same Harry, and Doris will not be the same Doris. And there will be more holes. Harry will hang out in bars with the other divers. Doris will spend her time at the track. Her horses never come in and she blames it on Harry. She thinks of him constantly, reliving the terrible moment when his snorkel vanished beneath the surface. Harry has forgotten Doris. He takes a booth at the back and drinks scotch and water with the other guys. He remembers playing beneath a sycamore when he was very small while his mother hung laundry in the meadow. He remembers being happy then. He knows there were no sycamores where he grew up and no meadow. He can't understand how he could have been happy then.

11. Chloe

So here they are again, with Manny on the bicycle and everyone else walking behind. Chloe especially is resentful at never being allowed on the bicycle. The people they talk to are not interested in their ideas. Chloe has knocked on more doors than any of the others. People everywhere are growing harsher. She doesn't enjoy standing on a doorstep pleading while Manny is doing wheelies in the street. The people don't even listen to her. They stretch their necks and stare past her, mesmerized by Manny. So of course resentment builds up after a while. She is losing faith in America. Sometimes she doesn't care if there is another war. They have a meeting every night. Chloe forms her own faction, but she is not a good leader. When she brings up the bicycle issue, no one supports her. Manny, riding with his hands in his pockets, circles her jubilantly.

12. Dorothy and Edwin

Nothing they care about remains. Packs of stray dogs roam the city. The dogs have gone back to being wolves. Swimming pools are filled with rainwater and weeds. It is not true that Dorothy still loves Edwin. At the end of a movie the filmstrip makes a clattering noise as it comes off the reel, just as it did in the old days. "We still have that," Edwin says to Dorothy. They are alone in the theater. No movie has been shown for weeks. It is icy cold in the theater. They have come in to escape the large dogs roaming the avenue. Dorothy often imagines a world of books, one with no dogs, no movies, and no Edwin. Edwin imagines Dorothy more like other girls, like the ones he used to see at pool parties, when it was still safe to go into the pools. He was too shy to speak to those girls then, and now they are gone. It is pitch dark in the theater. The only sounds are their own breathing and the far-off rattle of the guns. "They sound like a filmstrip coming off the reel, don't they," Edwin says to Dorothy, who snuggles closer.

13. Weather Report

If the sky stays gray we won't have fun today. It's no good walking by the lake. Looking out at the cold, gray water, our spirits will only sink lower. Our spirits are already lower than they were the day we stopped for lunch in Nebraska and your little dog ran away. I can barely remember the dog, though I remember clearly how I felt after he ran away. I felt guilty and remorseful. We should have separated then, right there in the parking lot. The people who live across the street are not attractive. I watched them leave this morning, coming down the steps of their house, under the gray sky. There in the parking lot, fighting about the dog, we were still young and attractive. We had that going for us. The sky was enormous. It was cloudless, the sun was huge and hot, the little dog was lost, and we were yelling at each other.

14. Ruins

Clyde and Ellen have driven in from the country to see the ruins. You can't drive all the way to the center, to get there you have to climb over miles of rubble. Clyde shows Ellen where the ancient colosseum stood. It was already a ruin, he tells her, before they destroyed it. There are other tourists there, picnicking some of them, and others hunting in the ruins for interesting pieces to take back with them. Though no one alive is old enough to remember the city, they experience these visits as a homecoming. Ellen has brought a little trowel with which to dig while Clyde keeps a lookout for animals. There are more animals, and more dangerous animals, than before. One day it will be impossible to come here, because of the animals. They are not sure what the city was for, why so much stone, steel, and masonry was piled up and knocked down, and whether the aim was building or destroying.

15. A Road Trip

The car was finished. They didn't know anything about cars and had no idea why this one had stopped running. After standing around for a while just looking at it, not even lifting the hood, they started walking. They were cheerful at first, making a fun adventure out of it, but they became cross as the day wore on. They weren't equipped for hiking, had never hiked anywhere before, they didn't have hats, and the sun was merciless. The road climbed steadily upward, and toward evening they arrived at a summit with a specular view of the road ahead of them. They saw mountains and more mountains. They had already drunk most of their water. Nothing in their past had prepared them for this. They should never have set out, they could see that now. They should have stayed home, they should have kept their jobs, they should have taken care of the children. They thought of the children, their tear-stained faces at the window, watching their parents, waving gaily, drive off in that jalopy.

16. The Colony

The planet is not satisfactory. The fact that it is larger than their native Earth means the gravitational force is greater. Everything is harder, just lifting one's feet to walk across a room is exhausting. Everyone is always tired. The air outside is toxic. In the beginning, people went outside exploring, a practice they abandoned generations ago. There is nothing out there for them. Between growing food and repairing machinery, there is not much time for the things that mattered back on Earth. Every year more people are needed to repair leaks in the dome. One day that will be everyone's future. In school the children are shown pictures of animals and waterfalls and sky and things like that.

17. 911

They were about to call the police when Carol urged them to think of Grandmother, of how frightening that would be for her. "Calling 911 is bound to just set them off," she said. Toby joked that maybe they should call lost-and-found instead, but nobody thought that was funny. Someone else suggested that, if they called 911, they should ask them to not bang on the door and shout, "Police." "Why do they always do that?" Carol wondered, looking down at Grandfather and nudging him with her foot. "Why can't they ring the doorbell like normal people?" "They are afraid of looking silly," Joel explained. "Imagine them standing at the door with their rifles and armored vests and helmets and all, the assault vehicle idling on the lawn, sharpshooters crouching behind it, and then pushing on the bell with one finger, when what they want to do is just shoot the door lock off." Gavin disagreed. He had flunked out of police academy but had come away with a deeper understanding of law enforcement. He said "law enforcement" very softly so as not to frighten Grandmother, in case she was crouching behind the door. They all agreed that she would die of fright if they shot the door lock off. "They were together sixty-four years and he had it coming," Carol said, and nobody could argue with that.

18. Rainy Day

There was nothing they could do to stop the leaks. The roof was forty years old. Stella's grandfather had shingled it himself the summer he came home from Vietnam. She barely remembered her grandfather. When it began to leak, Kevin got a ladder out of the garage and applied roofing cement to the broken shingles, but walking on the roof made leaks in other places. It was an old wooden extension ladder, probably the same one the grandfather had climbed when he was younger than either of them. They placed pans and bowls on the floor beneath the leaks and when it rained the drips made a kind of music. Kevin said it sounded like John Cage. Among the bowls was one Stella had found at a thrift store for a dollar. It was a beautiful bowl. The fact that it was sold for a dollar was testimony to the decline of taste that you could see everywhere now. Stella and Kevin were artists. They could see the beauty in a bowl like that and hear the music in a leaking roof, but they didn't know where to go from there. It was raining the day Kevin was looking through Stella's stuff and found the picture of her grandfather working on the roof, smiling down at the camera, so young and handsome. And it was still raining when he went into the bathroom and shot himself with the pistol she kept under her sweaters.

19. Home

They wondered whose dog that was. It sat on the porch and glared. This same house had housed them once, when they were small. There were other dogs then, small as well, and friendly. They held hands now, as they had then, and peered over the fence. They had come so far, they didn't want to turn back. They stayed till sundown and then drove to the motel and ordered pizza. Olives, anchovies, green peppers, and mushrooms. Celia picked the mushrooms off her pieces and gave them to Michael. Afterward, and after a shower, they sat side by side on the motel carpet. The master had said, "Empty your minds," but their minds were filled with anguish. They slept with the television on but the sound off, just to have the flickering light in the room. The next morning they drove away in a sandstorm. Michael fiddled with the radio as he drove, searching for something besides Mexican music, while Celia looked out the car window at houses and trees that were barely visible through the blowing sand.

20. A Twist of Fate

One bright summer morning, a man carrying a loaf of bread walks up the Rue Gassendi. At the corner of the Rue Daguerre, a young woman carrying a dozen ripe plums in a canvas sack falls in behind him. The plums are the small yellow ones known as mirabelles. She eats a plum as she walks, bending forward at the waist so as not to get plum juice on her clothes. The man shifts the loaf from his left hand to his right. He has not turned his head and noticed the woman walking behind him eating a plum. The woman has not noticed the man in front of her carrying a loaf of bread, first in one hand, then in the other. At the Avenue du Maine the man turns left, while the woman continues across the avenue and on up the street, which at that point is called the Rue des Plantes.

21. Rumors of Justice: Two Cases

I.

The judge asks, "Does the accused wish to make a statement?" The accused is disheveled, wild-eyed. He reaches in his pocket, pulls out a tightly folded paper, opens it with difficulty, and begins to read. His hands shake, his voice is barely audible. The men and women in the jury box lean forward, attentive. This goes on for several minutes before they realize that he is talking in a foreign language.

II.

Same situation. The accused takes a crumpled paper from his pocket, unfolds it, and begins to read in a firm, confident voice. He reviews the charges against him and then, with circumspection and diligence, attempts to undermine them point by point. The jurors stare into space, pare fingernails, glance at the clock, whisper.

22. The Machine

It's the same machine. They've just painted it a different color. The gauges are new, but the basic function is unchanged. We break it out of the crate and, after moving the lathe into the other room, set it up next to the old one.

We all want to work at the new machine. When I get home, Steve is drinking again. We have franks and potatoes for supper. The light falling from heaven is stronger than it used to be. Steve says ten, maybe twelve years, and it will all be over. Management will decide who gets the new machine. Once there were bus trips that lasted for days, when Steve and I would get down in little towns and stand by the bus smoking. We would watch the people going up and down in the little towns, and they looked contented and wholesome and we would talk about staying. Management has still not decided. The machine just sits there. The others pretend they don't care. I get home from work and Steve is standing across the street by the drainage pond. Someone has taken a red marker and written Zelda's name on the new machine. She says good-morning, and I can tell she is on top of the world. She throws the lever and grins. Steve announces there are ducks on the pond, where before there were only gulls. He is finding signs everywhere, but to me the ducks don't matter. If they had given me the new machine, I would be on top of the world. One of us has to keep her feet on the ground.

The Songwriter

There was a novelist who wanted to write a song. He wanted it to be a beautiful song like "Summertime" or "La Vie en Rose," a song for the ages, as the saying goes. The novelist had a decent singing voice, knew hundreds of songs by heart, had only to think of a lyric in order to hear it sung in his head, but he was not a musician, he was not even a poet. He wanted to write his song in prose, and his prose did not sing, it was harsh, satiric, and bitter. The best reviewers and critics, praising his novels, used words like *brutal, fierce,* and *merciless,* but the novelist hated every sentence he wrote. He completed many novels over the years, he had a coterie of devoted fans, but most people judged his books too harsh and bitter, and he lived out his life in poverty and died of a disease that like his prose was merciless and brutal. In his final weeks, when the pain was enormous and unrelenting, he refused the drugs the doctors urged upon him. He was a strong man without faith of any kind, and true to his life and art he was determined to greet death with a clear mind and eyes wide open. His last hours arrived, the friends and followers who had been keeping a deathwatch gathered at his bedside, shadowy forms that he could only dimly perceive. A gauzy film clouded his vision. He tried to rub it from his eyes but was not able to lift his hand. He closed his eyes. He could not hear the voices of those still trying to reach him, he saw only blackness. For what seemed to him hours he heard only the hollow sound of his own labored breathing. And then came the song, a single long intricate sentence of unspeakable beauty, the pain melted away, and a great happiness filled him. He opened his eyes wide, and staring at the faces by his bed, recited the song in a loud, strong voice, he said it over and over, it was so beautiful, he was handing it to them, his friends, his family, this precious thing, this great beauty. His voice was weak. He was breathing his very last breaths. The sitters came closer, they leaned over him, they strained to make out the words. His voice quavered, it was hoarse and less than a whisper, it rose and fell back and rose again, as if reaching for some final ineffable syllable, but it formed no words that any of them could understand.

Dispatches from the Commune

1.

Charles was in the yurt and would not come out. He had crept in at night when everyone thought he was sleeping. Despite the crooked smile and useless right arm, he could still surprise them. At supper the next evening, all eyes were on the empty chair. Jill, who was standing at the window, said, "He's still in there," and everyone felt glum. Beth carried a plate of food out to the yurt. She knocked on the door. "Go away," said a voice. Returning to the house, Beth reported that Charles sounded "subdued." In later testimony, she changed that to "muffled." She left the plate on the ground by the door and the next morning it was empty. They wondered what he was thinking about in there. They imagined him seated in the dark gnawing on a chop bone.

2.

Every night, one of them went out to the yurt and left a plate of food on the ground, and every morning, when they looked out, the food was gone. One morning at breakfast,

Beth came in from the yard carrying the plate, empty as usual, and Warren said, "Raccoons," and everyone's heart sank. The next night, Steve went out and put his ear against the side of the yurt. "He's chewing," he whispered. He tapped on the wall of the yurt and the chewing stopped. "He's eating. That's a good sign," Lily said, and they all brightened, until Monica reminded them that she had eaten like a horse right up to the day she had swallowed a whole bottle of pills after supper and they had had to pump her stomach out.

3.

"He went in there to send us a message," Rachel said, and they all agreed, though no one could think what the message was. Warren, who was interested in Zen, said, "Maybe it's the message of no message," and everyone nodded. They couldn't imagine what Charles was thinking, and that took them aback. In fact they had never known what he was thinking, even on his best days, but they only realized this after he went into the yurt because that was such a surprising thing to do. Charles, everyone agreed, was a closed book. "Enigmatic," Beth added, trying to be helpful. "He played his cards close to his chest," Marek put in, and they all glared, because that was the wrong tone.

4.

Charles had seemed such a reliable, predictable person. He had never done anything surprising before except for having a stroke, though Rachel said that this didn't count since he had been even more surprised than they were, and Lily said that it shouldn't have surprised anybody who saw how he ate. They had missed the warning signs, and now they blamed themselves. They all agreed that they ought to have known something was wrong when he dropped the flag ceremony. Beth recalled seeing him alone in the yard listlessly throwing rocks at the chickens. Ronald remembered the morning he had found him in the hammock reading *The Brothers Karamazov*. Everyone agreed that this was not like the Charles they knew.

5.

The flag ceremony had been such a comfort to him after the stroke. Everything he did was predictable until he went into the yurt, and the ceremony had come off every day like clockwork, Charles out in the yard at sunrise with the bugle. Though nobody else was fond of the flag, which they all agreed stood for things they could not approve of, they admired the way he had worked the rope with just his left arm and his teeth. Standing at the base of the pole, he had watched the flag unfurling in the morning sun. "There she blows," he would say every time in the most chipper way imaginable. They were supposed to stand at attention, but they just glared and slouched or refused even to come out of the house. It was the flag ceremony that had turned them against Charles.

6.

With Charles in the yurt, life was easier for them all. It was a relief not to have him popping up when you wanted to

be alone, making irrelevant comments while you were trying to think, insisting on games after supper, and saying,
"Roger that," when you asked him to take the trash out.
It was only now that they realized how tired they were of
his war stories. Weeks went by, and they didn't talk about
Charles as much as before. Sometimes when they were
having lunch at the big table under the oak, someone
might, in the midst of the revelry, glance over at the yurt,
and that would remind everybody that he was crouching
in the darkness there, and the conversation would flag
while they adjusted. The idea that he was listening to their
laughter frightened them a little. They slept with windows
and doors locked, not to be surprised again. He was still in
there when the police came. They pointed their guns at the
yurt and Charles crawled out. His hair was full of dirt and
leaves, and he wore an expression none of them could read.

Thespa

Sitting here I can see Thespa's cup, the cup from which Thespa drank coffee. I would like to say that I see a smudge of lipstick on the rim, though Thespa was not wearing lipstick. If I were to get up from the chair and go sit on the sofa, I would be where she sat while she drank the coffee. There is still a slight indentation in the cushion where Thespa sat. She is slim, but she is a womanly slim, and her buttocks have made a larger indentation than mine would, I believe, were I to sit there, though I am taller than Thespa. When I kissed her, back when I did that, she would tilt her head up to bring her mouth against mine, because I am taller. There has been a time, during the worst of it, when I closed my eyes and imagined kissing Thespa. Sitting where Thespa sat, were I to do that, getting up from the leather chair in which I am sitting, have been sitting for hours, and going over to the sofa, I could find out if she has left a little coffee in her cup, verify what I know already even without getting up from my chair, that she has not finished her coffee, because Thespa never finishes anything. She leaves behind, as relics of her passages, crusts of sandwiches, half-read novels, curdled milk, fizzed-out cola, starving cats, unsigned checks, unkept promises, inchoate projects, and questions hanging in the air like a last whiff of perfume. Were I to go over and sit there, sit next to where she sat, and place my hand on the sofa beside me, in the indentation where she sat, I might imagine still feeling the warmth of Thespa, though it has been hours since she sat there, and the fabric would be harsh and cold, like the absence of Thespa, and I would lift the cup and drink the last swallow of her coffee, which would taste of her breath.

By going over and sitting where Thespa sat, I would disturb a fly that is walking on the little piece of cake she has left on the plate next to her cup, a fragment of a small ingot-shaped lemon poppy-seed cake that I bought this morning at the bakery where I buy bread on Mondays and Thursdays. In the kitchen, conscious of Thespa waiting on the sofa to hear what I had to say, hands folded in her lap the way she always sits when she does not intend to listen, feeling her waiting as a kind of judgment upon me, as if only a fool would drag out this moment with coffee and cake, I sliced two small pieces from the cake and put them on matching white plates that I carried in with the two coffees on a lacquered wooden tray that is now on the floor next to the table on which the nearly empty cup and plate are sitting.

It is a rattan table with a glass top. The trees on the hill outside the tall window are reflected upside down in the glass. There are clouds as well, puffy white clouds moving softly across the surface of the glass, as they move across the surface of the sky. They must be upside down as well, though that does not seem to matter. Had I looked at the tabletop earlier, I might have seen Thespa there, walking away under the trees, upside down as if she were walking on the ceiling. It has always been like that, Thespa walking away across the ceiling of my world, though I never thought of phrasing it that way until now.

If I were to get up from the chair and go out the door and stand under the trees, I would be reflected upside down in the table as well. If someone were to come in while I was still standing there under the trees, a policeman, perhaps, summoned by neighbors, or the landlord wondering why the rent has not been paid, and sit where I am now sitting, he or she would see the empty cup and plate on the table, the lacquered tray on the floor, the small indentation in the sofa cushion, and a man upside down beneath the trees, weeping, but he (or she) would not know what to make of it, would not be able to supply the thoughts that belong to those things. Only Thespa can do that. If Thespa had come back while I was standing where she had stood, where she had paused a moment under the trees to look back at the house before turning again and walking briskly away, and had sat in the chair where I am sitting now, she would gather the objects, the cup, the plate, the lacquered tray, into her thoughts, the way she used to, in the evening, gather her book, her comb, her phone, her toothbrush, her shawl into her arms before climbing the stairs to bed.

It is almost dark now. The coffee table, the cup, the saucer are dimly visible. The fly is not walking on the cake crumbs anymore, and it is not on the windowpane. If I got up and went over, I might find it floating in the sweet brown puddle Thespa has left at the bottom of her cup, and where the fly, its wings wet and sticky, unable to climb the slippery wall of the cup, swam as long as it could before drowning.

I could also just leave the cup and the crumbs for other flies, for the maid who will come in two days and clean them up. She will come in and go directly to the kitchen, where she will take off her coat and drape it over one of the four chairs in there. She will go around the house gathering up the cups and glasses and carry them into the kitchen and sweep up the shattered glass in there. She will pick up the clothes Thespa has left scattered in the bedroom and bathroom and throw them in the hamper in the bathroom. She will do the dishes and vacuum. She will arrange the four chairs in the kitchen neatly at the four sides of the table before putting on her coat and leaving.

Wallflower

He had never learned to play anything, not a Jew's harp, not a ukulele, he couldn't carry even a simple tune, and the funny thing was, he didn't know this at first. Every morning in second grade, after the teacher had called the roll, they stood in the aisles next to their desks, placed their hands over their hearts, and recited the Pledge of Allegiance, and after that they sang "God Bless America," and he sang along with the others. He loved "God Bless America," he belted it out, and it sounded good to him then. He danced as well, in junior high, when they started having dances, and he was a terrible dancer. He moved the wrong way at the wrong time, stepped on toes, or collided with his partner, and after a while he decided that he didn't care for dancing. He would still get dressed up for parties, but once there he would hang out in the kitchen and talk with other boys. Sometimes he would stand by the dance floor and snap his fingers to the rhythm of a song, to show that he was having a good time, but he was often unsure— unsure of the rhythm and unsure that he was having a good time. A glance shot in his direction would fill him with anxiety, and he would push his hands deep into his pockets. Gradually he came to see that there was something wrong inside him, a failure of perception, a kind of blindness within him. His seemed to lack access to the vital and mysterious code that let others move effortlessly to music, and this lack, this blindness, made him incorrigibly gauche and awkward, and he was aware of that now, and he stopped going to dances and stopped singing in public unless he was drunk with friends. Later he wouldn't sing even then, he would just sit quietly by, bobbing his head and grinning. He would have given ten years of his life to be able to play an instrument, he would have done that happily, to be able sit on his front porch and pick out a tune on a guitar. He wanted to be the guy in the old movies who sits at a piano, hands dancing over the keys, while attractive young people crowd around, adoring him. The thing was, the really tragic thing was, he wasn't tone deaf. He was deeply moved by music. Brahms and Tchaikovsky brought him to tears, Mahler was so painful he sometimes couldn't go on listening and had to get up and shut it off. The tragic thing was he didn't know anybody who listened to that kind of music anymore, he had no one he could talk to about it. There had to be music inside him, if he had feelings like that, he was sure it was inside him, locked up in there, and he couldn't understand why it would not come out. Sometimes he thought maybe that was because he didn't have enough confidence, didn't truly believe in himself. He had played baseball as a kid, he had loved baseball, but he wasn't very good at it and they always stuck him in the outfield. If a fly ball came his way, he would say to himself, *I'm gonna miss it, I know I'm gonna miss it,* even as he was running toward it he would be saying that, he couldn't help it, and then he actually would miss it. Sometimes he sang in the car if he was out on the highway but never in town where people in other cars might hear him. Now and then there was a song he knew on the radio and he would sing along with it. It didn't sound so bad to him then, and he thought maybe that was because he was alone and not bothered by a lack of confidence. Same with girls. It was the eyes on him that made him feel so awkward. He couldn't just go up to a girl and start talking to her at a party. The only time he managed to do this was at a costume party one New Year's Eve, when he was dressed up as a bear. Talking to this pretty girl there, he forgot about the awkward person he was, he felt he was just this friendly, outgoing bear, and he could tell she really liked him. Concealed in the bear suit, he even danced with her, and his awkwardness seemed just part of his bear act. They met again later a couple of times, but it didn't work out. He could see she was bored, and the harder he tried to be entertaining, the worse things got. He couldn't get the bear personality back without the suit.

Ducks

They sent the ducks down the line and I stamped them. They were not ducks of course, not even toy ducks. And stamping also, there was no stamping. Everyone called it "stamping ducks" and I went along. I try to get along with people generally and have learned from experience not to call something one thing when they are calling it another, even if that is not what it is. It's just words. So I went along with the others and we all said they were ducks. It was easy work, even though I was thinking in the back of my mind that they weren't really ducks. I stood across from Tony and we stamped them. Down the line other people were doing the same. Most of the ones that reached us had been stamped already, but we stamped them anyway. To fight off boredom we played games. Tony stamped mine and I stamped his. We competed to see who could stamp the hardest. Sometimes we let one go by and then ran after it and stamped it. It was my first day. "Simple," the foreman said. "Here's a duck" (it wasn't a duck). He picked up a mallet and stamped it. "Now you do it," he said. I watched Tony until I got the knack of it. "Look, it's a duck," he said to me, and he grabbed one by its "neck" and shook it in my face. He was convinced they didn't suffer, or only suffered a little. Tony was a good sort, older than me, and years at the job had worn him down. "Another duck, another dollar," he would say when he hung up his mallet at the end of the day, even though it was not a dollar and they weren't ducks.

Cigarettes

My landlady stands in the doorway, one hand braced on the jamb, breathless from climbing the two flights of stairs to my room. She's come up to bum a cigarette. It's the same old story. Her doctor convinces her to kick the habit, scares the shit out of her, sends her home full of virtuous resolve. All she can talk about for the rest of the day is how she's finally quit smoking, how this time she really means it. The next morning, stepping into the kitchen, the first thing I see is her coffee cup on the counter, a couple of soggy butts disintegrating in the saucer. "It's not worth it," she says. "Next time I decide to stop, you need to tell me it's not worth it." I know how she feels, so I refrain from wise-cracks and just hand her one. She lights it, takes a long drag, and sighs. The smoke drifts from her mouth and nostrils. "Shit," she says. I twist my chair around to face her, tip it back against the desk, and light my own. We smoke awhile, not talking. We are two-packs-a-day smokers, the landlady and me. Same for her brother, Clement, who has a separate apartment in the basement but spends most of his time upstairs in the kitchen or in the living room in front of the TV smoking. Clement rolls his own. It's a house of smoke. One of us is always at it. Sometimes we are all three smoking at once, and the smoke gets thick as fog. There is a sticky film on all the windows. The landlady says there is no point wiping it off. There are not that many real smokers left. We are the last of a dying breed, Clement says. We stick together even though we don't have much to say to each other. They don't let you smoke in restaurants or bars anymore, so we never go out at night. Starting next year we can't even smoke in the parks. I remember when you could smoke in movie theaters. Same with friends. Nobody gives parties where you can smoke anymore, and if you drop in for a chat, they want you to stand outside in the rain to smoke, or in the freezing cold. Thrift shops are full of ashtrays that nobody wants anymore. If people have ashtrays, it's to hold paper clips and the like. So we spend a lot of time together—me, Clement, and the landlady, hip to hip on her little sofa, watching television and smoking. Of the three of us, Clement is the expert smoker. He can blow rings, one after the other. I can blow a ring now and then, but success is haphazard, and the rings are raggedy, not perfect Os like Clement's. He can't explain how he does it, says it's just a knack. I'm not upset that I don't have the knack. In my view blowing rings is not an important part of smoking. I told Clement he could piss off with his rings. I visited France when I was young, lived there for almost a year. France was a smoker's paradise in those days, but I was so down-and-out I had to buy the cheapest cigarettes. They were called Parisiennes. They came in packages of four and were so loosely packed you had to hold them horizontal while you smoked or the tobacco would fall out.

The bums, who were most of the customers for those cigarettes, called them P4s. I was in France for so long without cash that I was calling them P4s too. Nowadays the three of us spend most of our money on cigarettes. My daughter won't come to my place. Tipped back in the chair, facing my landlady, whom I don't particularly like, the two of us not exchanging a word, just smoking—that's as good as it gets. My daughter says she can't get the smell of cigarettes out of her clothes, even after several washings. I can't make her understand.

Sky

Let us go then, you and I,
When the evening is spread out against the sky
Like a patient etherized upon a table.

T. S. Eliot, "The Love Song of J. Alfred Prufrock"

I stayed in the car in the driveway while she ran back to
the house for a sweater. She ran, I noticed, heavily. Had
she not actually been running—and she *was* running—I
might have described her as *plodding* back to the house.
She doesn't run on her toes as she once did. She runs on
the flats of her feet. She doesn't, I reflected, run trippingly.
Were she not five foot two, I might have said *lumbered*. It
takes a certain avoirdupois to lumber, though, and while
she has definitely put on a few in recent years, I think it is
still O.K. to speak of her as *smallish*.

A smallish, chubby woman pretty well sums her up,
I guess. It is the description I would give to the police,
anyway, if one day she went grocery shopping and never
came home, along with the other bits they would want:
medium-length blond hair, hazel eyes, and so forth. "Any

distinguishing marks?" they might ask. "No," I would say. "None." Of course they would not be able to find her. Described in that way she could be practically anybody. Which is a thing I have begun to notice more often—I mean, how very *ordinary* she looks. I don't notice it all the time, just at odd, apparently random moments. This morning in the kitchen, for example, while she was staring into the refrigerator in search of the half-and-half. Another sign, I suppose, of falling out of love.

We are both approaching fifty—I think I need to say that. She has just turned forty-seven, while I am older by a smattering. She is Adele, my wife of many years, and I am Al. I feel uncomfortable saying it, saying, I mean, my wife of many years. We were on our way over to Paul and Linda's for supper, already backing out of the driveway when she popped the car door open. "Sweater," she blurted, and nearly fell out onto the pavement.

Paul and Linda have a house at the beach, on an island connected to the mainland by a causeway. We go there for supper every other Wednesday. Dining with Paul and Linda is invariably alfresco during the season, just the four of us squaring around a patio table at one end of a long screened porch. That is a soothing place to sit. It is soothing even when they are out there with me, facing me across the table or, afterward, sitting next to me in their wicker rockers. In the lulls in conversation, I can sometimes pick up the dry hissing of the surf beyond the vast expanse of white sand. At other times the wind rushing up from the beach makes an attractive whistling in the screen that drowns out even the creaking of the rockers.

The Plymouth was idling roughly, as usual, the engine speed climbing, then descending, then climbing again, desperately, like a dying person breathing, making the car wallow from side to side. I kept it alive with deft pats to the gas pedal. There was still no sign of Adele. Tiny needles were pricking my neck and shoulders. I distracted myself by randomly punching the buttons on the radio. The radio was broken, and the buttons did not make anything happen. And that was true generally. Of my life, I mean, it was generally true that the buttons did not make anything happen. Other than what usually happens, of course. Perhaps it would be better to say that there were no more buttons.

When we dine at Paul and Linda's, we usually take the same seats at the table. Mine has me staring down at the far end of their extensive porch. They have strung a new rope hammock there. I am, proximally speaking, facing Paul, but if I lean just slightly to one side I can see around him and get a good view of most of the hammock. Lean to the other side, and there is the rest of it. On windy days I become almost hypnotized watching it sway back and forth, back and forth, back and forth, to the point of losing track of what the others are saying, if they are saying anything. Sometimes, if Adele catches me doing this, she rests a hand on my knee, "rests it affectionately" is how it appears, and gives me a sharp pinch when no one is looking.

We had set out earlier than usual this time, to be there before the full moon was up. But now, with Adele still looking for her sweater, it was anyone's guess when we would get there. Linda and Adele and even Paul in his devious, backhanded way can still become excited by the moon, and Linda puts a lot of emotional stock in having us comfortably in place when it rises, so we can comment. I cannot for the life of me understand why this matters. At our age we have already seen so many full moons, along with others, gibbous, crescent, and so forth, and yet we continue to comment. *She* continues to comment, and *they* continue to comment. As for myself I don't suppose I have said three words about the moon in as many years. I sit quietly by, I look down at my plate, I stir my food into interesting shapes, while they expound on the moon's enormous size, its yellow hue, how it relates to the surrounding clouds, if there are any. After that they talk about real estate. Of the four I am the only one not connected in some way with real estate. I am not "in" it, as they say. I am "in" women's sports clothing.

I was sure she must have found her sweater by now. The night before, I had picked it up from the hall chair where she had flung it after work and had hung it in plain view in her closet. I remembered doing this because I had used the occasion to line up her shoes, which she leaves every which way on the closet floor. She must have continued on to the kitchen to check that I had unplugged the toaster oven and to refill (again!) Michelangelo's tray. Though I never in fact forget to unplug the toaster oven, she has to check. Adele worries a lot about going up in flames. I don't know what that comes from. We are the only people on the block without a gas grill, because she is afraid of burning down the house. So twice a week I sear our New York strip steaks in an iron frying pan, filling the kitchen with greasy smoke that has left a sticky brown film on the ceiling. A few days ago I noticed that it needed repainting, again! Or maybe she had found hairs on the sweater and was standing at the mirror picking them off. Michelangelo is half Persian.

I switched the engine off, producing the usual weird silence. I glanced over at the yard next door. Simpson was standing there like an oaf, his meaty fist wrapped around a gigantic black fork, next to the shiny apparatus he bought last spring. It looked like a small locomotive. White smoke was oozing from beneath the lid. He waved the fork in my direction, a slow, vague gesture, as if he were conducting an orchestra in his sleep. It was an odd incommensurable moment like a bubble of frozen time, as if everything were planning to stay just like this forever, I sitting in the car, in the weird silence, watching Todd Simpson move his fork back and forth. But then, without a sound, the bubble popped, and I was conscious of how silly I must look sitting alone in my car in the driveway. I leaned across the seat as if searching for something in the glove compartment.

I was leaning over, my head more or less sideways, when I noticed the sky. I had been staring absently out the windshield for the past five minutes or so without notic-ing anything particularly odd, so perhaps it was the fact of my eyes being now located one above the other that brought it into focus, the stereoscopy or whatever being slightly deranged in that position. It was not a particularly large piece of sky, compared to something like a desert or beach sky, probably not more than a couple of hundred square feet of it altogether, stretched taut as a trampoline between the two houses, our pale blue ranch and the white bungalow next to it. A few clouds of the cotton-puff variety were floating around in it (on it, actually, since the whole thing was quite flat and, as I said, taut), but not the parade of hippos usual at this time of year nor the long feathery smears from the whipped-cream dispenser we sometimes get when a cold front is coming through. In any case, the impression of oddness did not emanate from the clouds (the impression, I want to say, was quite emphatic on that point) but from the sky itself. I want to say, putting it now as precisely and matter-of-factly as I can, that the sky was extremely horizontal. I had the impression—put now, I admit, rather more breathlessly—that it was *lying down*.

"Why are you sprawled across the seat like that?" Adele shouted through the window. She was trying to open the car door. I was still half reclining across the seat, one hand forgotten in the glove compartment, the other grasping the armrest of the door she was struggling to jerk open. "Let me in! Let me *in*!" I sat up and discovered that I was clutching a map of Maine. She plunked herself down in the passenger seat. She looked straight ahead and noisily expelled a large amount of air. I looked at the map of Maine. I began backing out of the driveway. Simpson waved good-bye with his fork. I waved back. I was holding the map. Adele had something in her lap. It looked like a big bunch of black cloth. I thought I recognized her black angora sweater. One arm of the sweater had escaped the main bunch and was dangling over her thigh. She was wearing spandex jeans, and I noticed how thick her thigh was. Thick and short. Linda has long muscled thighs. Linda is thirty-five and works out every day. Adele never works out. She is forty-seven.

An hour later we turned off the coastal highway onto a county blacktop. We had entered open country, a pine-and-scrub-oak barren, billboards bigger than house trailers, house trailers on concrete-block pillars, metal garages, collapsing barns. It was the way I remembered.

We had not spoken since leaving the house. Still clutching her bundle she stared absently at the road ahead.

"Did you notice," I said, "the sky is sleeping."

"Yes," she said. "It has fallen asleep at last."

"What will happen now?"

"To us?"

"Yes."

"We will go to Paul and Linda's and have a few drinks and watch the moon rise. You will get quite drunk and make a fool of yourself, and I will go to bed with Paul."

"Does it have to be that way?" I asked.

"Well, it is hard to imagine it any other way."

She shifted uneasily in her seat, adjusting the bundle in her lap. It unfolded slightly. I caught sight of paws.

"Michelangelo," I said. "Why have you brought Michelangelo?"

"From now on it is going to be just me and Michelangelo. I am tired of your lassitude, your phlegm, your quiet obsession with women's clothes. I am sick of looking at interesting television shows while you sit with your nose in a garment-supply catalog. I feel nauseated when I come home from work and confront your head poking up from the wing chair and think, *How like a mouse he is.* Have you no *spunk*? No mettle? No gumption? I have brought Michelangelo because he has spunk pouring out of his ears. It's going to be me and Michelangelo. And maybe Paul. And maybe Linda. And maybe some other people too, if we can find them."

This was what I had expected her to say. After all, for a long time it had been Michelangelo this and Michelangelo that.

We drove on in silence. I said, "Our life together has been seized by lethargy, by ennui. We move like animals tangled in someone else's dream. It is like drowning in thick syrup."

"Yes. I have noticed. I have felt it in the advertising jingles you send to the radio. They ooze thickly and don't rhyme anymore."

"They never did rhyme."

"Perhaps. But they sounded like they rhymed. They were bouncy. It is many a long day since they bounced."

"A reflection of the times," I said. "They reflect the times. The times are without bounce, you cannot have failed to notice that. We have entered a period of inelasticity and lethargy. Though we trick ourselves with delusions of false dribble, the universe is bounceless."

My words gave her pause. We drove through marshland with bulrushes higher than the car roof. The tires sang a familiar tune on the newly surfaced asphalt.

She said, "Well. This is the end, I guess."

"Yes," I agreed. "This surely is the end. After you sleep with Paul, I will try to sleep with Linda. She will rebuff me cruelly with her wicked left, causing me to stagger drunkenly backward. There will be nothing left for me to do then but fall asleep on the rug in front of the television. Later you will leave Paul in the bedroom and come lie beside me while the television grows mysteriously louder. You will drag yourself over and try to turn it down but the knob will prove too much for you—"

"Al," she interrupted, "do you ever have the feeling that our lives are scripted?"

I glanced over. She was staring at the sky again. "Al," she said again. There was a new tension in her voice. "It's not just asleep. It's *anesthetized*!"

I declined to be deflected. "I will drag myself over next to you," I continued. "You will turn your face toward me. I will notice that the rug has left a pattern of little squares on your cheek. I will reach out and touch them. You will say, 'Tell me a story about a rabbit.'"

"I *won't* say that."

"Yes, you will. And I will say, 'Once upon a time there were four little rabbits, and their names were Flopsy, Mopsy . . .'"

She had turned away and was looking out the window. She had her hands over her ears. She was not listening.

"In the old days they called them conies. That's where Coney Island got its name. It's really Rabbit Island."

"Why don't you shut up."

We had left the blacktop for the long concrete causeway to the island. The tires sang an octave higher.

I resumed: "I am going to fall asleep on the rug, only to be wakened later by shouting. The three of you will be standing over me shouting. It will be four o'clock in morning. I will open my eyes just in time to see you throwing Michelangelo at Paul. He will sail with his four legs outstretched and land on Paul's back. They will make sounds of surprise and agony, each in his native tongue. Paul will sit down and Michelangelo will run upstairs. Everyone is going to feel very bad, and you won't be able to find Michelangelo for several hours. None of us will sleep. I will make another scene at breakfast."

"What kind of scene? I hope not a threatening one."

"Not very threatening. I am going to tell about the mermaids."

"The ones you heard singing?"

"Yes, singing each to each."

"That was such a long time ago. Are you sure you should bring it up again?"

"Do you think my hair is growing thin?"

"Yes, and your arms and legs as well. In a bathing suit everyone notices."

We slid to a stop in front of Paul and Linda's. Their house stands on tall piers with its front door fifteen or so feet off the ground at the top of a long flight of wooden stairs. Paul and Linda were leaning on the porch railing. They looked down at us and waved as we climbed out of the car. We smiled and waved back. Adele walked in front, carrying a sack-like Michelangelo in her arms. I watched her trudge up the stairs. Halfway to the top she turned and looked back, not at me standing at the bottom, a hand on the railing, but westward at the sky, looked, I want to say, wistfully. I glanced up at the bronzed down-tilted faces of our smiling friends. They looked sleepy. Adele had reached the top. I called up, "I forgot something, be along in a jiff." Strange, I thought—I had never said the word *jiff* before. I turned back to the car.

I did not, as I drove away, hear any shouting. I drove back over the causeway and onto the blacktop, dropping an octave. It was dark by the time I reached the open country of scrub trees and trailers. The full moon was rising. The sky had changed, but I couldn't tell if it had woken up or died.

Rita

When he thinks of Rita, he pictures her as she was then, though he knows that can't be right still. Sometimes, if he sees an attractive older woman in the street or grocery, he'll imagine that that is how Rita looks today, though the women are never as old as she would be now. He has no idea where Rita is. She might have come back to L.A. too, if things have gone badly for her. She was fond of L.A., despite everything. She could be dead for all he knows. Even if she has come back, they are unlikely to chance on each other. He once tried to calculate just how unlikely, but there were too many imponderables. For all he knows she is living around the corner. He is not sure he would recognize her if they crossed in the street. He would if he looked at her closely, but if she were just driving by in a car or sitting a few tables over in a restaurant, he might not look closely. Why would he look closely? She would drive on past or get up and walk out of the restaurant. He would never know they had brushed past each other. He feels sick when he thinks of that. He is not sure anymore about the picture he carries in his mind. It is not really a picture any-more, just an idea and a name. He wishes he had kept a photograph of Rita. He is not sure what shade of brown her eyes were. For all he knows she was standing behind him at the checkout last night. She might not have recognized him from the back. She wouldn't have expected him to have put on so much weight. On the other hand, maybe she noticed that a guy in front of her was buying Heinekens. Maybe she remembered that he always drank Heinekens. Maybe she looked closely then. Maybe she knew all along that it was him in front of her, and still she didn't say anything, because the pain is alive for her too. Sometimes he thinks the pain will never stop until he finds her. If he could talk to her just one more time, if they could sit down together and really talk for once, then maybe he would find out they have nothing in common anymore. He has thought about putting an ad in the newspaper or hiring a detective to look for her, just to find out if she is still alive. He sometimes has a weird kind of daydream. He is in line at the checkout. He turns around and she is standing there just as she used to be, as if there were no such thing as time.

My Writing Life: A Confession in Fable

I want to say, this is how it was. I want to believe that this is how it had to be. I don't want to rebel against fate. What could be more pointless than that? So I go on, thinking always of stopping. I lay myself down to sleep, on the pavement or in the leaves, and vow to stop tomorrow. I wake up and begin to scribble again. It's not that I have so terribly much left to say, it's that I have nothing left to say. I listen into myself, to the noises within, the whistling and muttering.

I would like to have silence. I remember a teacher who would whack her desk hard with the flat of a ruler and shout, "I will have silence!" I will have silence. A silence within, genuine and profound, with which to meet the silence of the end, assuming there is an end.

The noise is like the sound of wild animals sometimes or of machines or otherwise inhuman things like wind in pines and surf on rocks, and at other times it is like the sound of old people in rockers or children at play or whispering together or weeping in some dark place they've been sent to for punishment, and I sometimes imagine I could tolerate all the others if I could make those stop.

So I go on writing, laying down one sentence after another. I lay them down like sponges hoping they will soak up the noise, the howling, the mumbling, the creaking, the chattering, that they will become swollen with the noise, grow fat on the absurdity of the noise, and come to an end.

I lay them down in a little notebook that fits in my shirt pocket, with a pencil stuck in beside it. In the other pocket I have a little sharpener for the pencil, for when it gets dull from scribbling, though worse even than scribbling for dulling a pencil is the crossing out, which I do with vigor so as to totally obliterate the thing that was there and is not wanted anymore, in case anyone should have a desire to look at it.

The current notebook, the one I write this in, has forty-four or forty-eight pages, I'm not sure, I counted them and forgot. I am not meaning that it still has forty-four or forty-eight pages, but in a recent past, no more than ten days ago, it had the one or the other, though it has only seven now, as I have just discerned by counting back from the end.

When I have finished a page, I tear it out and throw it away, which is why in the current case, having reached page seven, counting from the end, I can't say whether it is—or was when I first put pencil to it—a notebook of forty-four or forty-eight pages, counting from the beginning.

When I have reached page nine, counting from the end, I buy another similar notebook, which I carry in the pocket with the sharpener. That being so, and having been so for years, it follows that there are periods of time, hours or even days, when I carry a notebook in each pocket of my shirt, or to be precise, a notebook in one pocket and the remains of a second notebook in the other.

I don't carry an extra pencil, I have learned from experience that I will only lose it. When I have just one pencil and it is lodged in my mind as the only pencil, I am careful to clap my hand over the pocket when I run, or pick up something off the ground, or lean forward for the flush lever, or otherwise bend over, tempting gravity in those various postures, which, while they hold risks for the notebooks as well, the danger is less, as the notebooks are firmly wedged between the two layers of cloth that make such a thing as a pocket, and the sharpener lies deep at the bottom of one of them.

Having a second notebook, still unsullied, as I think of it, in the other pocket keeps a great weight off my mind and I am able to go on my way with a glad step and only the thicket of words to trouble me.

I have been going a long time, and stop only to sleep and to eat, and to relieve myself in an alley or behind a tree, though sometimes I eat while I walk, and lately to rest on a bench or a rock, or just sitting on the ground or on a fallen log if I am in the woods and there are logs, or in the leaves if there are no logs, and sometimes I sleep in the leaves and sometimes on a bench, and when it rains I don't sleep at all but stand hard against the wall of some public building to get shelter from its roof, and I otherwise stop only when the urge to press my little pencil to paper is more than I can bear.

It comes upon me all of a sudden, and I stop in my tracks. Stop in my tracks psychologically speaking, as I am, as often as not, already stopped corporeally speaking in one of the ways I mentioned, sitting or standing, when the fit comes upon me, or am in transition between one posture and another, or am leaning against a lamppost, gasping for breath, or have already slid down the post to the ground and am lying on the pavement, too weary to go on. I sit up or sit down, depending, extract the pencil from my pocket, and, if the point seems dull, sharpen it by sticking it firmly into the little tapering hole in the sharpener and twisting. I remove the pencil, flick the shavings from my trousers briskly, and stifle a little sob as I recall the way my mother, on her knees in the cottage doorway, used to brush breakfast crumbs from my suit with a straw whisk before sending me off to school. I take the notebook from its pocket and open it on my knee. I ponder a moment, staring blankly before me. I bend over, place my face close to the page, and set down whatever thing has been nagging at me. And that done, I resume my journey with a new spring to my step, and I might even swing my arms as I go.

Before I was in this place, I was in another place that looked almost the same. I had come to that place looking for my Molly. I was always hoping for a glimpse of her, and sometimes the hope would set me imagining I had seen the image of her reflected in a window glass or winking up at me from the bottom of a stream, as happened once when the thought of her came upon me while I was peering over a bridge rail. I once thought I saw her on a bus and ran after it shouting for it to stop, but it rolled on and left me choking in the dust.

The second place is so like the first that if I did not remember leaving the one and traveling to the other, and sleeping by the roadside, and traversing a vast plain without any houses or signs of life except cattle, and if a building in the one place were not blue while in the other it was red, I would swear I had gone in a circle and come back to where I started.

Molly wasn't in the first place, no more than she is in this place, but I stayed in the one and now in the other because she travels and is as likely to come to where I am as to be in some other place I might go to.

It was fear that got me started, fear and loneliness, scribbling on scraps of paper I found lying by the road. I knew nothing of notebooks then or of the orderly production and disposal of dreams and memories, but I was well on my way, having always a fat wad of paper scraps stuffed in a pocket.

On a good day I can still get the mind clear enough that I can have my daydreams, think about the days with Molly or my home with the parents, the little I remember. I push away the other things that are always clamoring at me, begging to be thought about, elbow my way through them and get up close to the window glass, so to speak, and with a bit of my sleeve rub a little hole in the dirt and grime big enough to peer through, and I see, as in the oval frame of an old photo, a picture of the parents, stricken with age and bent, standing side by side in the cottage door, the brothers and sisters crowding in the hallway behind them. The parents always appear to me in that ancient way, when I get them in focus, though they could not have been very old when I left. Truth be told, in the course of my wanderings, what with the erosions of time and blows to the head, I have lost the actual memory of them and have in its place constructed a picture of them out of sundry bits and pieces I took from the cottagers and crofters, so to call them, that I encountered on the road, and that is just as well, as I have been going for a long time and they are old now, if they are still in the world with me, which is not likely.

It was easy then to imagine I was just going out for a play day and would return in the evening to the cozy place I had set out from and where, after all, I really belonged. They stood in the doorway, and I with my bicycle, my biking helmet, my toe clips, reached across the handlebars and shook the hand of each in turn, beginning with my father. I mounted the bike and lurched up the hill, wobbling and tottering on the loose stones of the path, while behind me rose a din of farewell. My mother wailed as if I were being lowered into the grave, the brothers and sisters clapped and jeered, the dogs barked, even the cows and sheep let fly a chorus of lowing and bleating. I had nearly reached the high road when I looked back and saw that my mother, a little aproned figure far down in the valley, was out in the pasture waving her handkerchief.

I reached the open road and fell in with the traffic. Whole villages were on the move in a turbulent press of vehicles and conveyances; donkey carts and pushcarts and bikes mingled with claxoning transports, taxis, prison vans, and bright-painted buses. Contents of entire houses swayed in mountainous piles on drays and wagons, with sometimes a tethered cow lumbering at the rear of a cart or a huddle of sheep trotting after. Choking on the dust of my fellow travelers, I bent over the handlebars and pedaled furiously, plunging into what I thought of as life's great adventure.

It had seemed, viewed from the safety of childhood, so much fun, and yet it wasn't, and after a good many years I saw it had not been the right thing after all, though of course by then it was too late. One of the aspects of the great adventure is the impossibility of revision. That is, so to speak, the tragic aspect. There were bad choices at the beginning, and bad luck, a bad leg, a lost bike, blows to the temple, tendencies to inebriation and sloth. They warned me there would be no second chances, but I trusted to luck and soldiered on. The problems came in part from the imperfect view I had at the outset. I was, after all, still young, the field of action, if I may call it that, was enormous, the goal obscured by something like fog.

I was young and trusting and it seemed to me that so many people going in one direction would be going that way with some purpose, though none could tell me what it was, and whether they were fleeing something or seeking something, I didn't know, but I saw no other way, and for a long while I followed the traffic and ate their dust, and each time I came to a new place, I would look around me and say, "Here I am at last," and then discover I wasn't. And yet I blundered on, in plain view of the mountain of carcasses, so to speak, of others who had made the attempt before me. I don't remember how long I fared in that manner, my memory is a rusty sieve, but I know that my bike that had flowed smooth as water when I set out now squeaked and rattled as it went.

After a time, seeing no prospect in that direction, I turned aside and chose smaller roads, and sometimes not roads at all but footpaths and rutted lanes, walking and pushing my bike and sleeping by night in woods and fields, and I saw nothing but farms and small towns and vast empty spaces. The nights were cold and if I was not near a habitation where I could seek shelter in a barn or beneath a hayrick, I built a fire in the woods and lay down beside it.

I seldom met other travelers, or so it seems to me now, though perhaps I met a great many and even became friendly with two or three to such a point that I was sorry to part from them, but have forgotten them since, as seems more likely. But I seem to recall one who came upon me all of a sudden, walking out of the night to where I sat huddled in a blanket by a fire I had built at the edge of some water, though whether that was in a lake or ditch I can't recall. He was a pale, dusty beggar of a man, and he looked half-starved, though I don't otherwise remember his particulars, except that he had a funny way with his cap, which he would take off when he spoke and clap back on his head the instant he fell silent. He sat on the other side of the fire from me, his knees drawn up to his chin, and I seem to recall a lively conversation with a great deal of back and forthing and a corresponding quantity of doffings and donnings, but if he told me his name I have forgotten it, and if I told him mine he was the last to hear it.

Whether the cause was the tediousness of the conversation or the warmth from the fire or the weariness from the long road, I dozed off where I sat. Alerted by a rustling at my back, I opened my eyes to see the stranger towering above me and holding a great long log, and before I could lift my arm or speak he had heaved it in the air with his two hands and brought it down on my head.

When next I opened my eyes, the sun was up. I rose, braced myself with one hand against a tree so as not to fall down again, and felt myself all over. I discovered a painful big lump on my temple and another on my crown. I looked around, but my attacker was nowhere to be seen. In the mud of the road, I saw the marks of his footsteps coming up the one way and the marks of my bike wheels going off in the other.

I had lost my bike, and the several blows to my head had knocked great gaping holes into my memory. I was in confusion, not able to recall the particulars of my journey, where I was intending to go, or why. Standing there in the muddy road, I stared down at the wheel marks and took stock of the fact that I had either to stay where I was or to go, and so I went. And once I was in motion, I had to go this way or that, and having no memory of my destination, or the life path I had marked out for myself, I followed the tracks of my bike.

For a long time I had no other goal than to follow my bike. Sometimes I lost the tracks after a rain or when I struck a bit of pavement, but I soon found them again, though whether they were the tracks from that bike or some other I couldn't know, and it was the same to me either way. One day was like another. Free to go on, or free to stay, I went on, driven by the boredom that overcame me when I stopped any place for long, looking about me at the same trees and rocks. And once I was going I went in the direction my bike had taken, and while I walked, I thought about this and that, and as there was nothing on the road to ponder but bushes and rocks and such that were, as I said, similar from one day to the next, I was led to recollect what I could from my past, and in the course of rummaging in the bygones, I discovered a great many gaps and holes and other such punctures and perforations where something must have been in my head that had gone missing. I couldn't recall the name of the place I had come from, the number of months and years I had been gone from there, the names of my brothers and sisters, or how many I had of the one and the other.

I went a great many miles in this way, in pursuit of my bike, and what with the coming of warm days, the emergence of green leaves and flowers, the pleasure of breathing deep and steady and putting one foot in front of the other, I was loose and carefree. The only cloud in the sky was not knowing my name. I had been going a good long time without it before I noticed it was missing, as I saw nobody and was not in the habit of addressing myself in that way. At first the knowledge that it was gone gave me a chill, and I sat on the ground and hugged myself and felt afraid and alone. But soon enough I saw it was no good disjointing my head in search of it, and I rose and went on my way, thinking it would pop into my mind one day, and in the years since, a great many names have turned up in that place, but whether one of them was my old name is impossible to say. I would dub myself with this one or that one, as the occasion demanded, when ordered to do so by a policeman, the several times I was accosted by one of those, but none of them had the air of belonging to me and none of them stuck. Molly named me Ned, saying, "You look like a Ned to me," but whether she chose that name on a whim or because she had an inkling of the truth, I never found out.

She had glossy black hair and dressed like a Gypsy and had arrived in that town with a band of musicians that traveled in the wake of a circus. We met on a bridge in a park, she going one way and I the other, and we stopped in the middle to gaze on the swans.

At first I was carefree and happy. I strolled in the streets with Molly on my arm, and I felt the envious eyes of other men upon us. I called her my little wife, and we talked together of a cottage in a valley with flowers in the window boxes and children at play in the fields.

But I was still aching with some kind of hunger, though what it was for I couldn't decide. I squinted and peered into the darkness, as it felt to me sometimes, and shaded my eyes against the glare, as it felt at other times, but never got a view of it in the one way or the other, and whether it was too close or too far I couldn't make out. And Molly walked behind me in the streets, the sun flared and ricocheted from every tree and building, while I wandered in a tunnel of darkness, in the hollowness of that yearning, straining toward nothing I could name.

Molly would play little tunes on a harmonica, and I would close my eyes and let the pictures come and go. I would wake in the night and listen to her soft, peaceful breathing in the bed beside me, and the thought of the open road would fill me with longing and terror. She had a little flashlight that she kept on a table by the bed, and I would make shadow puppets on the ceiling with my hands, and struggle against the anguish that was sprouting up in me, until the batteries grew weak and the figures on the ceiling faded, and the bulb became an orange glow and went out. I would shake Molly awake, and we would sit side by side on the edge of the bed and smoke and talk until the rectangle in the wall began to gray.

Every morning, the moment she rose from bed, my Molly would go over to a calendar that hung from a nail by the window and stand awhile just looking at it. Because it was the morning after the day before, if it was Wednesday, the calendar would say Tuesday. After a good long time contemplating it, she would reach up and tear the page off and say, "Well, that's that," and throw the page in the trash can. She said the same thing every day, and whether it was my fancy stirred by the knowledge of time passing, or whether there was really a gradual change in her voice, every morning the way she said it seemed to me sadder than the day before.

And so it went for that long while, with the fine days getting fewer and the bad days getting worse, until she finally had her fill of me, and then one day the tents of the circus were folded, the clowns shouted up from the street, and Molly ran down the stairs and went with them.

I walked up and down in the little towns and the big ones, up to the logging camps and down at the river ports, looking for her. Some people remembered a circus having been there, but that was long ago, and others remembered it was a carnival or a freak show, and others said it was a traveling opera company. I went to those many places and never found her, and the places came to so resemble one another that I wasn't sure, walking up and down in the one, that I wasn't wandering in a memory of another, and I would become confused and stop people and ask for the name of the place, and they would say sometimes this and sometimes that, as if they didn't know themselves where they were, and if they didn't answer anything and just walked away, offended by my looks or my manners, I would get angry and curse them, and if they had given me money, I would throw it back at them.

As I went along I would formulate my thoughts as best I could. I would chant them aloud or say them over under my breath, to prevent them from sinking out of sight and coming back later to torment me. I was sorry I had let Molly go, and I wrote her a letter expressing how I felt, where I promised to do better, though I knew it was a lie. But I had no address to send it to, so I carried it in my pocket for a good long while, and finally tore it to bits and threw the bits away, and that was how I got started.

That was a great many years ago. I am old and Molly is old and I might not know her if we met, but even if I did know her, passing her in the street one day, and she did not know me, I would not turn back and speak. It's no use thinking I would turn back and say, "Molly, don't you know me?" I have thought of many ways the conversation might go after that and none make me want to begin. What's finished is finished.

When I came to the first place, looking for Molly, I was writing on scraps and dropping them on the roadside, half thinking that she would pick one up and know that I had come that way. And it happened a few times that a policeman saw me tossing away a morsel of paper I had picked up, scribbled on, and dropped, and made me go back and pick it up again, and it was useless to explain that I was only returning the paper to where I had found it, putting it back, I would add, augmented and improved with ponderings and musings and bits of verse. So I would walk back, as slowly as I dared, and pick it up and stuff it in my pocket, disposing of it there temporarily, and when I had gotten a ways off and was hidden by the corner of a building or some bushes, I would pull it out of the pocket and throw it away again, permanently for the most part, though it happened once that there was a second policeman, and while I was picking the paper up again under the eyes of that one, the first policeman reappeared, and while I was stuffing it back in my pocket for the second time, the two of them stood off a little ways with their caps together and discussed my case. They must have seen that I was old and perhaps not right in the head, for all they did was make me pick up all the paper I came across in the street for two or three blocks, which I was glad to do, while one of them strolled behind me whistling and twirling his baton.

The policemen in the place I am now all know me, and I keep a distance from them. If one of them finds me asleep in a spot where I can be stumbled over, presenting a hazard to the public, he will poke me awake with his nightstick.

There was a time, when I was younger, when policemen amused themselves by making music on my head and ribs with their sticks, but they've tired of that since and are satisfied with a few sharp pokes to the ribs, which I don't much mind, and I always oblige by moving off in whatever direction they indicate, and am careful to thank them for pointing me the way.

Even before I met Molly I hadn't known where I was going, but after she went I began to suspect that wherever it might be I wasn't likely to get there. All that time I had been looking for my life path, and now it was dawning on me that there wasn't one, that my life was destined to be just a foolish meandering and a roaming around and about until there was no more strength left for it and it stopped. So I have taken my direction from the wheel marks of a bicycle, mine or another's, it hasn't mattered, from the traces and rumors of Molly in this place or that, and lately from the proddings and nudgings administered by guardians of the law, and one way of going seems to me as reasonable as another.

But I am weary now of going up and down and swinging this way and that and the oscillation of day and night and the swerving of my mood from merry to somber and back again. I don't fear the end, I fear instead that death won't be the end. I want to believe that life is like a bright light, and when it goes out it leaves nothing behind, but what I fear most of all is that I will wake up from death to the same life again, and eat the same apple and sleep in the same bed and walk the same road and love Molly again and lose her again and there will never be an end of it, a kind of hell, a torture, not because it is painful but because it goes on, because it won't ever stop.

There was an inconvenience to using scraps for my writing, apart from the fact that there might be none lying about when the urge came upon me. They were frequently of irregular shape, most were printed all over and useless for writing, and the rest had served for wrapping food and were greasy and stained. They had often been wadded and crumpled into tight little balls in preparation of being thrown, in which case I had to spread them open on a surface and rub them smooth with a flat stone that I carried in a trouser pocket for that purpose. As often as not, there was no suitable surface at hand, and by the time I had found one and had rubbed the wrinkles out, I had lost all trace of the bothersome thought that had prodded me to pick up the scrap in the first place, and it was these inconveniences that led me to the idea of carrying a little notebook of a size that would fit in my pocket, so as always to have a morsel of clean paper handy.

Of the notebooks I possessed in the past, some had forty-four and some had forty-eight pages, as I mentioned before, but I never knew, at the moment of purchase, whether I had got the one or the other, the fat or the lean, and so the first thing I would do on leaving the shop was stop in the street and count them. There was a flaw in the manufacturing process, but I couldn't determine whether, as a result of the flaw, I was getting four pages fewer than I ought or four pages too many, and whether, if the count was forty-four, I should go back to the shop and complain, or, if it was forty-eight, be off with a skip and whistle. That is the way it has always been with me, never knowing whether to count my blessings or curse my fate, waffling between happiness and despair.

When the count of remaining pages reaches nine, as I also mentioned, I buy another identical notebook, which I carry in the pocket with the sharpener. Having it there means that if I am caught up in scribbling when I reach the bottom of the last page, I can let go of that one and grab the next with scarcely a break in the orderly transcription of the chittering and drumming in my head.

Before I had gotten into the habit of carrying an extra notebook in the other pocket, I was, on reaching page nine, counting from the end, accustomed to walking back to the shop where I had bought it, to buy another, and with nine pages left I was able to stroll in that direction with a tranquil mind, confident of my goal, taking a roundabout path to gawk at the sights, even stopping to rest along the way.

It was a cold winter morning, the air flecked with snow, so I had not dawdled and had all nine of my pages still intact, the day I discovered the shop locked tight and dark, and, according to a notice posted on the door, set to remain in that state for three days to come. I tried to get through those days, I bore up as best I could. Clasping the pencil in fingers numb with cold, I made my letters small and I scrunched the words so tightly together I could scarcely read them myself, but by the evening of the second day, there wasn't a whit of space left, and any scraps I might have picked up and used instead were buried under the steadily falling snow, and I fell back to mumbling and chanting, until finally I couldn't bear it any longer and nothing remained but to knock out a pane with my shoe, which I did, and I was standing in front of the store leafing through a notebook to see if it had forty-four or forty-eight pages, when a policeman came up and gave me some pokes with his nightstick and showed me the way to the jail, where I remained a good long time before I was, with the aid of several more pokes, ejected from that place in turn. I vowed I would never again venture into a place as devoid of suitable surfaces for bringing forth my thoughts as a prison, and I haven't, and to that end I have made certain to have a notebook in the other pocket when I need it.

When a page is covered top to bottom and side to side with scrivenings, I draw a big X across it with my pencil, and I say to myself, "Well, that's that," and then I tear the page out, and then I throw it away, in the manner of Molly disposing of our days. And sometimes, in place of an X, I strike out the words by drawing a thin line through them. But struck through or x-ed over, the writing stays legible, should anyone care to read it, the x-ing and the striking signaling more my own relinquishment of the bit of life I have pressed into the words than any attempt to conceal them. I leave them legible out of vanity, I suppose, or loneliness, imagining as I walk along that somewhere behind me someone will pick up the page from where I threw it.

Other times, I cover the page with a dense crosshatching, so the writing is hard to make out, and I think that a person reading it, if there is such a one, will be looking at my soul through the wire of its cage, or the other way around, that my soul is peeking out through laced fingers at the mystery of the world.

Most often, though, I take the pencil in my fist, and, moaning and cursing furiously, scribble all over the page until it is thoroughly blackened. I regret the times I was unfaithful to Molly, or cruel to her, and it would be a weight off me to blacken those pages, but I can't anymore.

When I have finished a page, filled it top to bottom and side to side with scribblings that I have crossed out in one of the ways described, or blackened, I remove it from the notebook by a series of gentle tugs, neatly severing it from the little line of stitches that anchor it to the book. I am careful to keep a rein on myself while I am tugging and not give way to the frenzy of impatience that surges within me at the prospect of a final and utter obliteration of my thoughts, and claw or tear it out. Performed correctly, the gradual sundering leaves the remaining pages firmly in place, but if my emotions get the best of me and I claw and tear or otherwise snatch at the page, I can weaken the armature of the book in such a way that the other leaves drop out of it. The stitches fly open and the pages escape, fluttering and tumbling to the ground at my feet. As often as not I am still occupied with the disposal of the page, blackened or otherwise, that provoked the frenzy, and fail to observe what has happened. Sometimes, if there is a breeze, the pages are already scattered about in the street, if that is where I am, by the time I notice, under vehicles and so forth, or they are fluttering in the air and sailing over walls and hedges, and I have to run after them, or, if I am not in the street, I might have pressed them into the mud with my shoes. Having recovered all the loose sheets I can, I stuff them in a pocket, with all the inconvenience that follows on this the next time an urge to scribble over-takes me—removing the wad from the pocket, extracting a crumpled page, replacing the wad in the pocket, smooth-ing the sheet with a stone, and so forth. In my extreme agi-tation I have on occasion thrown away the empty covers, hurling them into some inaccessible place, into the river once, down a street drain another time, and as a result had nothing to press on while I wrote, and was forced to make do with whatever hard surface I could find, a tree or a bench, rough surfaces not suitable for writing, and ended up driving holes in the paper with the pencil point, and with the usual consequences—shredding, balling up, and so forth. Once, after attempting to write on a page I held up against a sycamore, I flew into a rage and bit my pencil in two and hurled the pieces from me. Five minutes later I was crawling about on the grass looking for them. The sun was setting, the grass was damp, I could scarcely see the ground in front of me and was feeling about with my hands, when I finally touched one of the pieces, the shorter one, scarcely big enough to grasp between thumb and forefinger. After pocketing that bit of pencil, I discov-ered I had lost the sharpener, and I had to get back down on my knees and grub about for it half the night while cursing myself for not keeping a leash on my temper.

Sometimes I simply drop a severed page, let it flutter to the ground at my feet or sail away on the wind. Other times, depending on my mood, I fold it into a little packet, or I crumple it and roll it between my palms into a tight little ball that I am able to hurl a good distance from me, and sometimes I tear it into fragments.

When I have torn out a page and disposed of it in one of the ways described, I feel I have made a little progress, though toward what I can't say, and whether it is really progress and not regress or just standing still, I find impossible to discern, the jumble and jangle in my head being the same as before, but for a moment or two there is a great weight lifted off me.

Having removed, excised, and on occasion annihilated a page of my scribbles, I ought to be quit of them, comfortable in the thought that there have gone words and sentences I won't have to write again in this life, but it never works that way, and as I go along I mull on the fate of the pages I have abandoned along the way, that I have left lying in the road or in the grass in a park or in a field, bleached by the sun, dissolving in the rain, buried by snow, caught by a wind and blown with the dry leaves into gutters and streams, gathered by street sweepers, mingled with food wrappers and newspapers, discarded with the other refuse, stepped on by the polished shoes of strolling policemen, trampled by sheep, and so forth.

Sometimes, when a page strikes me as exceptionally poignant or amusing, I mark it very lightly with an X, just enough to show that the author, to wit myself, regards it as finished, and then I place it in such a way that someone, meaning some stranger, not Molly anymore, is likely to come across it. I place it, for example, on a park bench and, if the day is breezy, anchor it with a little stone, and then I hop off a ways and hide. Most of the ones who come to sit on the bench don't seem to notice the paper, or they sweep it to the ground with a careless gesture in order to sit in the place where it was, or they carry it over to a trash bin. But now and then it has happened that one of them takes it up and reads, and even turns the page over to see the other side, and on those occasions I have waited until he or she, more often she, gets up to leave, and then I run ahead for a little ways and turn and walk back to meet her, and I peer into her face as we cross, looking, I suppose, for a lingering trace of what she might have felt while she was reading, some small mark of sympathy, a tiny flutter of lips or eyes expressive of a fellow feeling that I like to think of as the faint dawning of love. But the result is always the same, her expression is inscrutable, and after we pass, I going one way and she the other, I feel more dejected than ever, and I regret having let my hopes get the best of me. I sometimes can't stop myself from imagining a young woman, someone of the age Molly was, finding the page and being moved to tears, and then I want to kick myself for a fool. A few times, from my hiding place in the bushes or behind a tree, I have watched people carry a page away, in a pocket once, and at another time in a purse, but whether it was because of the things I had written on it or because of a reluctance to litter I couldn't tell.

I have tried many times to throw away the notebook and the pencil and the sharpener with them, to be free of them for good, but I have never been able to carry it through. I have tossed them into bushes, hurled them over a wall, buried them in leaves, and walked away, and kept on walking for miles before turning back, strolling back slowly at first, then running, overcome with panic, terrified that someone has made off with them in my absence.

But they are always there, just where I threw them, of interest to no one. I pick them up and put them back in their places, notebook and pencil in the left shirt pocket, sharpener in the right, and I make a promise to myself never to be parted from them again.

The Adventures of Kiffler Wainscott

1. Kiffler Fails to Fly

Today Kiffler is learning to fly.
He has developed a technique.
He does it in the kitchen first for his family.

Fists in armpits,
he flaps the mighty stubs.

        Wugh wugh wugh

The sound of wingbeats
strums the air.

Once around the room,
he soars above the refrigerator.
Kiffler is flying the Hump.
He is sailing above it all.

The kitchen,
     his family,
         his life

shrink.

They are the size of fleas.

Now he is going to do a barrel roll.
(Impressive, but irrelevant.)

He is just fluttering up there to avoid his
responsibilities.

He crumples once more upon a chair.

"You don't have anything it takes,"
observes Thelma.

Does she mean wings?

From Molly's box of Jungle Crunch
a tiger recommends that Kiffler crunch life.

He would, he would.

"I leap up to my God, who pulls me down?"
said Dr. Faustus in that play.

And who is Dr. Kiffler leaping up to?

Nobody.

Then what drags *him* down?

His heavy heart.

2. Kiffler Sets to Work

Six long weeks he strove to cut it.
Thirty mornings at the awful hour
Kiffler stood panting at the door.

"Climb aboard," they said.
He climbed aboard. He hauled,
he hammered.
They called him Kiff.
His heart warmed.

Six weeks he did it.
At the end of each
lay money. Kiffler
was bringing home the bacon.

That was on the surface.

Elsewhere,
upon a barren piece of windblown prairie,
Kiffler was recoiling.

From ladder tops he surveyed
the passages of clouds.
Under houses in the cool
he contemplated joists.

He was happy there.
The word *deadbeat* fluttered in the air.
It lit on Kiffler's head,
and stayed.

He let his mind drift.
Day by day the name *Kiffler*
grew synonymous with *slacker*.

Six weeks he strove to cut it.
To what avail?

Down the street by Jimmy's Bar and Grill
lies the answer.

That rakish figure of springing step
is Kiffler fired.

Home again, he creeps
into the warm, familiar lair.
He wags.

With Thelma, though, that does not cut it.
"I put up with shit," she says.
"Why can't you put up with shit?"

Why can't Kiffler put up with shit?

A flaw within.

3. Kiffler Takes a Walk

The young ones are everywhere. They are
falling from the trees. They are leaping
from rooftops.

They are not doing anything. They do it
passionately.
The park is full of them.

Overhead the vastness reverberates.
A huge orb is loose in space.
Someone has let Spring out
and the dogs are at it.

Alarmed, Kiffler roams.

Tiny leaves on the willows.
Tulips and daffodils.
Gnats vibrate in columns.

A mallard, green aglitter,
pursues a drab wife,
all dignity undone by the waddle.

See Kiffler smile.
His teeth are quite yellow now.

At the lake's rim he sits,
knees drawn up to his chin.
(The body hinges,
the mind unhinges.)

He read this morning,
"Poet Allen Ginsberg Dead."
That news is now writ large
in Kiffler's head.

Once, hunkered in Asia
Kiffler heard a temple
gong so loud the whiskey
frolicked in his glass.

Now he looks to windward.
From across the lake
toward him and toward him
tiny ripples race.

If tomorrow Kiffler
woke up as a duck
that would be all right with him.

4. Kiffler Takes a Sort of Stand

Beached upon a sofa, mighty Kiffler rests.
His eyes are shuttered against a sea of troubles
even as trouble creeps upon him.
Into a quiet-breathing nostril
Molly jabs a note from school.

> Kiffler unfolds, and reads.

Molly has (it is written there)
refused to pledge allegiance to the flag.
She has alleged "parental strictures."
She has quoted Kiffler to the class:

> "You will not kiss their fucking rag."

Here Kiffler beams.
She has his vent verbatim.

Though he knows it's a skirmish only
(a footnote merely)
in the Kiffler Wars,
he swells with pride.

Propelled by wrath
he hauls himself erect.
Up from the well of resentment
he lifts a bucketful
and spews a bilious stream
down on Molly's hapless dome:

>   the *misery* of his schooldays.
>   the *shame* of his nation.
>   the *stupidity* of power.
>   the *fragility* of justice . . .

thoughtless thoughtless

Here Molly weeps

and Kiffler tumbles back.

—

Time tumbles forward,
carves Kiffler a narrow space
in which to rue and mend.

With ice cream in cones
and her small hand in his,
father and daughter amble now
beneath the flowering trees.

     Cunning Kiffler
     has made his escape again.

He bears the cone before him like a torch.

—

He's back where he belongs at last.
He never should have left.
He has his feet on the dog again.
His eyes are closed.

He is waiting for Armageddon
to be announced on the news.
He can hear Thelma singing in the kitchen.
The days are very long.

After a while, he rolls a joint
and wanders out to the yard.

He stands among the things of April,

     the tiny leaves that swarm the ash,
     sudsy clouds bouncing in the sky,
     daffodils, of course.

He takes a long toke,
coughs once, and pledges.

5. Kiffler's Nice Day

A nice day again.
Sun-speckled sidewalks,
flowers, and so forth.
Kiffler can't get over it.

An amazing coincidence
himself and the world
here together.

Amazing just to shirk. If he had anything
to shirk from. Or off.
There's an itchy buzzing
sort of bounce to the atmosphere.

        Kiffler takes Vachel to scope it out.

A slow turn around the neighborhood
and then amble on to the park,
and the lake, and ducks probably.

People have planted all sorts of flowers
between the house fronts and the sidewalk.
Thelma does that. Kiffler himself would not,
though he is grateful.

He doesn't know even the names of many.
Zinnias, roses. But what are those
yellow spotted ones
like tiny shoes hanging from strings?

Vachel meets others of his kind
on the way. He wags and means it.
And Kiffler meets others of his.

Does he wag? He does.
The doggy virtues do not elude him.
He bobs and nods.
He flashes a ragged grin.

That is just Kiffler being devious.

The sign says

NO DOGS ALLOWED IN THIS PARK.

But there goes Kiffler.
He's walking Vachel right past it.

At the leafy shore, eager
paddlers gather round.
They know their man.

Deliberately adjacent a sign that says, in effect,

DON'T FEED THE FUCKING DUCKS, KIFFLER,

scofflaw Kiffler tosses bread.

Minor crime is Kiffler's crutch.
Leaning on it he hobbles home
with head held high, high-domed

forehead slicing the soft air,
a man of backbone and gall,
unlulled by weather.

6. A Laborious Story

This is Kiffler as a large, fat beaver.
Fat, flat tail. Nice sturdy teeth. Incredible house.
Underwater entrance and other defenses.
Nice airy rooms. Roof deck with retractable awning.

Never a wasted moment, that's Kiffler.
Works hard. Strong as a mule. Never touches sugar.
Here he is singing "Down at the Pond"
while stripping off some fresh bark for the winter.

> "There's no such thing as too soon,"
> he likes to say. "And the busy bee has no sorrow."

Naturally, the other good-for-nothing beavers don't like
    him much.

They spend a lot of time just lying around chewing twigs
    and sunning themselves
and they don't feel good about it.

> So they organize a meeting to throw Kiffler out.

They accuse him of being an Eager Beaver.

"Yeah, I'd call him that."

"Some kind of militant self-starter
probably."

"Well, I did peek inside his lodge once, and lemme tell ya,
it was *neat* as a *pin*."

"With him it's always go go go. I say, when's
it gonna stop?"

He hasn't a chance. The case
is stacked against him from the outset.

They are out for Kiffler's pelt.

When his turn comes, he stands to speak.
He invokes the Beaver Way.
Industry. Self-reliance. The ideals
of the bluff plain dealer.
The sturdy yeomanry of yore.

He goes on, and on. His speech is extremely boring.

They drive him out with sticks.

Now here he is out in the big world.
It is a thinner, sadder Kiffler,
scrounging nickels in the street.

He is selling little wooden carvings of beavers
and singing "Down at the Pond."
He is in constant danger from dogs.

He has certainly traveled a long way from the old oomph
    and pizzazz days.

At night he drags himself home
to a hovel of planks and tar paper.
The only light is from a flickering screen.
Hunched over the keyboard,
he is composing the story of his life
and an indictment of his times.

(Beaver or no beaver, it's the same old Kiffler.)

7. Kiffler Has Mechanical Problems

Here is Kiffler hard at work.
Today he is an automatic high-velocity envelope-stuffing
    machine with bulk feeder.
He is amazingly efficient.
He is making up for gazillions of hours he has twiddled
    away.

> He likes being a machine.
> Effortless labor. Respect.

Buoyed by the warm chatter of office girls
he is humming along.
Envelopes are piling up.

Thanks to Kiffler thousands of deserving Americans
will have a shot at a free lawn tractor.
Just mail back the coupon.

Who does he think he's kidding?

Already he is losing his concentration,
he is drifting into orbit.
He is orbiting 1978.

Uh oh.   Something's not right.
Looks like a paper jam.

Here comes Janine to the rescue.
What a babe. She is fooling around inside
his very delicate mechanism
(long red nails like talons).

Hey, girl, not so rough.

Kiffler grabs, holds on.
Her shrieks merely excite him.

Oops! There goes the fabric.

"You've done it this time.
Out you go, buddy."

Here is Kiffler being unceremoniously
tossed.
He lies in the alley on his side.

He breathes. He hears the unpleasant
clatter of some loose parts.
He rolls over, studies how blue the sky.
Soon the bars will open.

Hands in pockets, he strolls to one.
"Hey, Kiffy, what's up, man?"

       Sly Mona Lisa smile.

He must be hatching another goofy idea.

When Kiffler was younger
he was troubled by the meaning of life.

          He felt there ought to be one.

He has gotten used to things as they are.
If one day they start to make sense
he will be completely bewildered.

8. Kiffler Tries to Sleep It Off

Kiffler is back on the sofa.

        What a deadbeat.

Kiffler Bonaparte
is retreating from something bigger than Russia.

      He does it with his eyes closed.

Outside lurks the work world.
(One more thing to be baffled by.)

It's a busy business out there,
he thinks, even the birds sound busy,
and Kiffler Doolittle hears it all.

He does not want to.

He turns, snuffling, to snout the pillow.
Deep in feathered folds he grubs for sleep.
Eyes shut tight, it is dark in Kiffler's head,
but sounds leak in.
From high in some leafy top
a small bright bird is shouting

phoo-ee phoo-ee phoo-ee.

He wishes he had earlids.

It's a busy, busy world
and Kiffler Bumstead is tired of listening to it.
He is tired of traffic and the busy buzz of people going places
in cars,
            subways,
                        buses,
                                    planes.

He hates business
and business people

and the phrase *travel allowance*.
He hates the words *busy* and *buzz*.
He hates the reliable, industrious
steps of the mailman
and the racket made by the painters across the street
ratcheting their eternal ladders up and down.

Their names are Ken and Laura.

Kiffler knows.
When they first started
he strolled over to find out.

Ken, Laura, and yellow.

Ken, thin and balding,
Laura, short and pudgy.
Laura does not actually paint.
She works as ballast. When Ken
is up high on the ladder
Laura sits on the bottom rung
and keeps him from falling.
All day she sits, eating potato chips
and smoking. That's her job
and she's good at it.

Kiffler thinks of slim Thelma
sitting on the bottom rung of his ladder.
She has kept him from falling
all these years.

But what is he doing up there anyway?

He ponders. His shield is down.
Wormish thoughts, tentacled and fanged,
wiggle into his half-sleeping head.
He wishes he had a mindlid.

And now another familiar tread.
No baleful mailman this.
The lighter, brighter steps of Thelma
are at the door, and through,
and across the room to him.
She looms above.
His eyes will open to behold.
O Thelma.

Has she brought bread?

Once she lavished
sex and praise upon him.
Now she returns
bearing, he hopes, money.

Kiffler needs some.

To sit with coffee,
pastry, perhaps a book
on a cafe terrace
and so stalk the world in spring.
That a need so small

should loom so huge
amazes Kiffler. Amazes also
that gentle, lovely Thelma
should labor so for such as he.

Baffled Kiffler doesn't get it.

When, Thelma asks, as she peels
away two lovely green ones,
will he face up to his responsibilities.

He ought to cry out, "Never, never, never, will I,"

but answers instead, "Tomorrow."

(And means it.)

9. Kiffler Treed

Bent beneath a long metal ladder,
there is Kiffler trudging across the lawn,
an ant bearing a wasp wing.

The summer trees are full of leaves.
Kiffler, below, has seen a better world up there,
a tranquil peace house afloat in the treetops.

He wants to go live in it.

Though he does not like ladders
he scurries up.

The vast maple waves its leaves gently to him
as he climbs.
His ant-heart thumps.

Now that he is in the branches
he starts to feel better.
Looking down, he is feeling high.

He climbs from limb to limb.
He is really way up there.
He perches near the peak.
Never mind how it sways,
he is going to make a roost of it.

But what's happening now?

Looks like his arms have gone furry.
Chest and face too.
Perplexed, he scratches a hairy ear.
His hand is huge.

Poor hopeful Kiff,
he imagines he's beginning a new life
story.
He wants to call it *From Ant to Ape.*

When he left, the news of the earth was grim.
High above the demented present
Kiffler is cutting loose from his species.

What will he miss?

Thelma and Molly, his sofa;
movies, his dog Vachel
cigarettes; wearing a hat when it's cold;
cappuccino on Cafe Zoma's terrace.

Kiffler is getting ready to rough it.

Now Thelma and Molly are standing beneath him in
the yard.
They are quite low and stubby.
Kiffler is so high he can't tell if they are pointing or waving.

From within his greeny nook
he peers out over the rooftops.
He has never seen the neighborhood
from this angle before. He likes it better.

Meanwhile
below him on the lawn
dwarfs are multiplying. They are wearing
their faces on top of their heads.
Friends and relations, all the neighbors,
his brother Bill, his sister Maud.

That's too much of many for Kiffler.

They are moving into a huddle.
Uh oh. It might be a family council.

Put a cork in that!

Kiffler hurls his shoes down,
first one, then the other.

The dwarfs unbunch and scatter,
then regroup out of range.
They are hatching plans to get him down.

        Kiffler studies his new feet.

He is up there
because it looked so nice from below
and he couldn't think where else.
Now he discovers
that sitting on branches is not comfortable.

The life of an ape-man
has turned out to be uncomfortable and boring.

        (There goes another illusion.
        How many more can Kiffler have?
Zillions, probably.)

The sirens arrive, trailing red trucks,
to die away at the curb. At the end
they give off a deep, very final moan.
If Kiffler could open his mouth and say *that*
everyone would understand.

Firemen swarm below.
Big-hatted, short-legged, barrel-chested,
they are running around with their fireman equipment.

DWARF ARMY RESCUES ORANGUTAN.

But why aren't they setting up any ladders?

The fire captain is explaining to Thelma:
When she called, they thought "Kiffler" was a cat.
They don't rescue lunatics.

They have a special team for that.

LITERATURE
is not the same thing as
PUBLISHING

Coffee House Press began as a small letterpress operation in 1972 and has grown into an internationally renowned nonprofit publisher of literary fiction, essay, poetry, and other work that doesn't fit neatly into genre categories.

Coffee House is both a publisher and an arts organization. Through our *Books in Action* program and publications, we've become interdisciplinary collaborators and incubators for new work and audience experiences. Our vision for the future is one where a publisher is a catalyst and connector.

Funder Acknowledgments

Coffee House Press is an internationally renowned independent book publisher and arts nonprofit based in Minneapolis, MN; through its literary publications and *Books in Action* program, Coffee House acts as a catalyst and connector—between authors and readers, ideas and resources, creativity and community, inspiration and action.

Coffee House Press books are made possible through the generous support of grants and donations from corporations, state and federal grant programs, family foundations, and the many individuals who believe in the transformational power of literature. This activity is made possible by the voters of Minnesota through a Minnesota State Arts Board Operating Support grant, thanks to the legislative appropriation from the Arts and Cultural Heritage Fund. Coffee House also receives major operating support from the Amazon Literary Partnership, the Jerome Foundation, McKnight Foundation, Target Foundation, and the National Endowment for the Arts (NEA). To find out more about how NEA grants impact individuals and communities, visit www.arts.gov.

Coffee House Press receives additional support from the Elmer L. & Eleanor J. Andersen Foundation; the David & Mary Anderson Family Foundation; Bookmobile; Fredrikson & Byron, P.A.; Dorsey & Whitney LLP; the Fringe Foundation; Kenneth Koch Literary Estate; the Knight Foundation; the Matching Grant Program Fund of the Minneapolis Foundation; Mr. Pancks' Fund in memory of Graham Kimpton; the Schwab Charitable Fund; Schwegman, Lundberg & Woessner, P.A.; the U.S. Bank Foundation; and VSA Minnesota for the Metropolitan Regional Arts Council.

The Publisher's Circle of Coffee House Press

Publisher's Circle members make significant contributions to Coffee House Press's annual giving campaign. Understanding that a strong financial base is necessary for the press to meet the challenges and opportunities that arise each year, this group plays a crucial part in the success of Coffee House's mission.

Recent Publisher's Circle members include many anonymous donors, Suzanne Allen, Patricia A. Beithon, the E. Thomas Binger & Rebecca Rand Fund of the Minneapolis Foundation, Andrew Brantingham, Robert & Gail Buuck, Louise Copeland, Jane Dalrymple-Hollo, Mary Ebert & Paul Stembler, Kaywin Feldman & Jim Lutz, Chris Fischbach & Katie Dublinski, Sally French, Jocelyn Hale & Glenn Miller, the Rehael Fund-Roger Hale/ Nor Hall of the Minneapolis Foundation, Randy Hartten & Ron Lotz, Dylan Hicks & Nina Hale, William Hardacker, Randall Heath, Jeffrey Hom, Carl & Heidi Horsch, the Amy L. Hubbard & Geoffrey J. Kehoe Fund, Kenneth Kahn & Susan Dicker, Stephen & Isabel Keating, Kenneth Koch Literary Estate, Cinda Kornblum, Jennifer Kwon Dobbs & Stefan Liess, Lambert Family Foundation, Lenfestey Family Foundation, Sarah Lutman & Rob Rudolph, the Carol & Aaron Mack Charitable Fund of the Minneapolis Foundation, George & Olga Mack, Joshua Mack & Ron Warren, Gillian McCain, Malcolm S. McDermid & Katie Windle, Mary & Malcolm McDermid, Sjur Midness & Briar Andresen, Maureen Millea Smith & Daniel Smith, Peter Nelson & Jennifer Swenson, Enrique & Jennifer Olivarez, Alan Polsky, Marc Porter & James Hennessy, Robin Preble, Alexis Scott, Ruth Stricker Dayton, Jeffrey Sugerman & Sarah Schultz, Nan G. & Stephen C. Swid, Kenneth Thorp in memory of Allan Kornblum & Rochelle Ratner, Patricia Tilton, Joanne Von Blon, Stu Wilson & Melissa Barker, Warren D. Woessner & Iris C. Freeman, and Margaret Wurtele.

For more information about the Publisher's Circle and other ways to support Coffee House Press books, authors, and activities, please visit www.coffeehousepress.org/pages/support or contact us at info@coffeehousepress.org.

Sam Savage is the best-selling author of *Firmin: Adventures of a Metropolitan Lowlife, The Cry of the Sloth, Glass, The Way of the Dog,* and *It Will End with Us.* A native of South Carolina, Savage holds a PhD in philosophy from Yale University. He was a finalist for the Barnes & Noble Discover Great New Writers Award, the PEN/New England Award, and the Society of Midland Authors Award. Savage resides in Madison, Wisconsin.

An Orphanage of Dreams was designed by
Bookmobile Design & Digital Publisher Services.
Text is set in Arno Pro.